The
Juan Doe
Murders

The Juan Doe Murders

A Smokey Brandon Mystery

Noreen Ayres

Five Star
Unity, Maine

Five Star First Edition Mystery Series.
Published in conjunction with Tekno Books and
Ed Gorman.

Cover photograph by Corbis

Set in 11 pt. Plantin by Al Chase.

Printed in the United States on permanent paper.

Library of Congress Cataloging-in-Publication Data

Ayres, Noreen.
    The Juan Doe murders : a Smokey Brandon mystery /
by Noreen Ayres.—1st ed.
        p. cm.
    ISBN 0-7862-2897-0 (hc : alk. paper)
    1. Brandon, Smokey (Fictitious character)—
Fiction. 2. Forensic pathologists—Fiction. 3. Women
pathologists—Fiction. 4. California—Fiction.
I. Title.
PS3551.Y74 J8 2000
813′.54—dc21
                                              00-061031

Out here,
killing's always in season.

> Walter McDonald, in "Black Wings
> Wheeling," from *Rafting the Brazos*

"You can't lean on nothin' up here,"
Philomene told him. "You gotta go
around like a little cat."

> Robert Stone, from *A Hall of Mirrors*

CHAPTER 1

I'd say the girl was seventeen. I'd say she had been pretty.

Now her forehead shone with an alien bulge, the left cheekbone was a pile of pink pulp, and a bite mark arched across her left eyebrow and mirrored under the eye. Covering her pubis and right leg was a twisted sheet. Welts flowered her ribs. Where the nipple of her left breast should be was only a red smear.

It was a Monday at the end of February, and the air was crisp and clean and the sunlight sharp enough to shatter. I'd parked in front of a murky-green house in a tree-lined, blue-collar section of Orange County fifty miles south of L.A. My silver-haired partner, Joe Sanders, lifted our evidence kits from the trunk and handed me mine. We crossed the street to the address we needed, where a sheriff's investigator in plainclothes stood talking to a Hispanic man in a white T-shirt and dark pants whose hands were cuffed behind. At the side of the lawn near the house a city cop in blue uniform parted bushes with his baton.

A deputy on the porch signed us in, then pulled open the screen door with screws missing out of its curlicued guard so it flapped with the motion. The mesh itself was a fractured design of punctures and tears. Inside, the odor of death met us; not strong, but unmistakable.

The living room was dark except for sunlight leaking under tinfoil applied to the windows with masking tape. A warren of sleeping bags and blankets covered the hardwood floor. Tipped against the wall on a fireplace mantel was a rendering of a haloed Christ with hands outstretched in benediction.

A deputy came out of the kitchen. He looked like a wary ferret, hard-faced and wiry. Joe knew him, but I didn't. When Joe said "Smokey Brandon" by way of introduction, the deputy's eyes narrowed. "I've heard of you," he said, as if trying to recall where.

Joe tried to deflect: "Some of us go for the fame and glitter. Others go for the glitter and fame."

"Aren't you the one . . ." the deputy said, "the one used to be a . . ." then caught himself before finishing.

"I'm the one," I said, matter-of-factly. "Want to show us what we have?" He gave me a second glance, then led us down a hall.

The window shade in the first bedroom was rolled partway up, revealing a bare twin mattress on the floor. A Styrofoam ice chest was topped by a brightly colored kiddy radio, the kind you get for a cheap hamburger plus 99 cents. Three ragged couch cushions formed another bed on the floor, and lumps of blankets and personal belongings lay along two other walls. "This must be the master suite," Joe said. "Radio. Refrigerator."

The deputy said, "Somebody's coming who can habla bean-ola. Investigator Bright's trying to get something out of him right now."

"The guy on the sidewalk," Joe said.

"Yeah, him. He's messin' his pants. He was peekin' out a car window, back seat. Thinks I don't see him, shit for brains."

"Who phoned it in?" Joe asked.

"White guy, two houses down. He come over to pay one of these tacos twenty bucks he says he owed on something. The door was open, six in the morning. Finds our scene here and gets to keep his twenty bucks one more day." Deputy Martin led us down the hall again, stopping at a door to the right. His arms hung away from his sides as if his lats were too big, cobra stance.

A second deputy came up behind us. High school would have been where I'd put him by looks, but he had a wedding ring on. Deputy Martin didn't offer introductions. "Here you have it," Martin said and stepped inside, holding his flashlight on the interior. The second deputy's gaze roamed everywhere but straight ahead.

Joe stepped in first and lifted a forefinger to the empty socket in the center of the ceiling. "Can we get some light here?" The younger deputy went off to scrounge a bulb.

As the deputy passed the beam over the red contusions on the girl's waist, arms, and exposed thigh, Joe leaned in for a closer look, his hands shoved in his suit pockets. I began a sketch of the placement of the body and the items in the room, noting an open cardboard box, a dark belt, and a ball of white nylon cord partly covered with a paper plate.

Joe straightened, closed his eyes, and walked by me and out into the hall, a strange expression on his face. I was about to follow when Deputy Martin said, "Looky here," and spotlighted a mouse backed into a corner alongside the cardboard box with clothes trailing out of it. "One mouse bound for heaven." He drew his baton to move on the animal.

"Thanks, Deputy, we'll take it now," I said, and held out a hand for his flashlight.

He shrugged and gave it over with a grin. "You're not going to be climbing a chair and shrieking for help, now are you, Smokey?"

"Stay tuned," I said. I tapped the cardboard box with the flashlight. The mouse leapt straight upward, darted along the baseboard, halted at the doorway, then sprinted through. I looked out after him and saw Joe leaning against the wall in apparent thought.

The younger deputy came with the bulb, Deputy Martin screwed it in, then left, saying if I needed his help to roust more rodents just holler. He squeezed by the videographer, Bob Hammerly, arriving to shoot both still shots and video, as I went to join Joe. "You okay?"

"Yeah, why?"

"You look funny."

"That's kind of you."

"What do you say we get out of here? The heater's on in the living room, that's why it's so hot," I said. Out of here meant only the front yard, because Joe wouldn't leave a scene early even if all of California was doing the tectonic-plate rumba.

We stood under an avocado tree laden with shiny boat-shaped leaves. A dead one slipped free of its mooring and glanced off Joe's shoulder.

"She was in there a lot of hours with people sleeping in the other rooms," he said. "Where are they?" His skin normally has a flush to it, heightened by hair the color of dimes, but he looked pale and I mentioned it. He said, "Ulcer, what you want to bet?"

I answered, "I think it's leprosy. Probably that."

"Sweetheart, I am circling the drain."

A bird cut in front of us, grabbed broken twigs from under a hedge, and zipped back to the eaves of the house. We walked to the edge of the lawn and looked down the street, deputies nodding or waving to Joe. After two decades at the lab, Joe seemed to know everybody, new employee or not.

On a block-wall fence bordering the next house sat two boys old enough to be in school. Their solemn eyes watched us and followed the low-flying birds tracing patterns from shrub to eave. One boy picked up a piece of broken capstone that lay atop the wall and gave it an underhanded pitch, hitting the tail feathers of a bird in flight. The bird let loose of a strand of nest stash but managed to lift off anyway. Then the boys scrambled out of sight on the other side.

As we walked back toward the house, Joe said, "Know what the worst is?"

"Sunday, and no ball game?"

He shook his head and almost smiled.

"Cookies, no milk?"

As if in any moment he'd spot the killer in the deep-green junipers that brushed at window-level around the house, Joe stared ahead and said, "The worst is," he said, "you can't un-know what you know. You can't un-see a picture."

Back inside, we set to work swabbing blood spatter, dusting for prints, and boxing up those items better examined at the lab. All the while, Joe was quiet, not joking as he often did.

Soon another lab tech named King Davis arrived in the ID van, with the coroner's van just behind. A small man, bald except for a robust ring of gray hair around the dome, King was as quiet as he was determined to get the job done and move on to the next. If he just worked fast enough, we kidded him, one of these days he'd close the gap between his arrival and the crime's commission so that he could claim eyewitness to a murder. We left as King was wrapping the mattress the girl had lain upon in plastic, to take it, whole, to the lab.

At the car I glanced at Joe as he came up on the passenger side and saw him put his hand to his stomach and wrinkle his face in a way that had nothing to do with sun.

By Tuesday noon the girl from the shoebox house in Santa Ana had been identified as an illegal named Nita Estevez. "Nita" for Juanita. The runt hiding in the car was one of the people who slept in the house, paying a hundred a month to do so. He worked graveyard shift at a mailing company. That morning when he came home from his job everyone had already scattered and the girl was in the condition we found her. A nice girl, too, he said. Made him sick to think about it.

Investigator Will Bright gained a thumbnail history of Nita Estevez. Six months ago she paid a cousin a thousand dollars to sweep her along a hazardous route from a little border town in Mexico to opportunity in the U.S. La Grullita was the name of the town; translation, Little Crane-just below Yuma. She was ushered in to work in a Garden Grove garment factory, making tank-tops for women and swim trunks for men at a wage that should but doesn't shame the sweatshop owners.

It took a few days for the news to reach the girl's mother through a series of calls from the morgue to the Border Patrol, Mexican police, and friends of friends. Now Mrs. Estevez had come to claim her daughter's body, using most of the money her daughter had sent home which she had been saving for the only child of hers who would get to go to high school, *this* year, because of Nita. I was at the morgue for a meeting about a different case when Mrs. Estevez was shown the photo that would serve as official ID for her deceased daughter.

From my vantage point, in an office across the hall, I watched her take the photo in her hand, suck in a long breath and turn a peculiar greenish color. She dropped the picture, rose from her chair, and walked stiffly to the side door, batting aside a young male companion's hands extended in solace. I excused myself from the meeting and went after her, but she was moving fast and rounded the corner to the front of the building before I got to her. Her companion jogged up to me, and the two of us watched helplessly as she cried *"Asesinos!,"* then plopped down hard on the sidewalk, leaned to one side, and vomited into the flower bed.

Years ago when I first became a cop in Oakland, I studied criminal justice textbooks, read department case histories, and listened to the brief or embellished tales from cops, the lies and truths from punks, the stories from emergency teams, and the anguished cries of victims' relatives. As a consequence, I grew alert to the way ordinary people talk to one another in violent phrasings, to the unthinking vocabulary of mayhem we all use: killer this, hammer that, tear his throat out. Placid scenes in others' eyes-a park, a trail, the beach at dusk-signified danger zones to me. Self-murder, war murder, murder in all the degrees. Through its study, I soon saw that in no way can man's imagination exceed his capacity for killing. Every contemplated method for exacting agony has at some time or another been proficiently, even proudly, performed.

Murder, big and small. This was my obsession.

After a while a certain peace settled in, as if by owning murder's gravity I could face all other things down.

I was young then, mid-twenties. Ten years have passed, and I am no longer obsessed. Then there was Nita. In my off hours I grieved for a girl who came looking for work who found death instead, who would never walk on perfect sand and smirk at seagulls, nor lift a child to feel a peach on a tree. Never would she move to the magic of music, enjoy the inexpressible touch of a lover, or thrill to challenges within her own mind, and I wanted someone to be held accountable;

someone. For the violated girl in the Santa Ana hovel, I would do my part to render justice.

Yet I knew the primary burden of solving this case was not mine. I'm not a sheriff's investigator. I'm a forensics specialist in a buck-strapped, shorthanded county crime lab where, after a county bankruptcy, layoffs continue, retirements are urged, and the concept of hiring seems archaic. This crime was not even as bad, one might say, as the surpassing brutality of those against children or the elderly, if one can put a scale to the gravity of murder.

But Joe was right—you can't un-see a picture.

I wanted the killer of the young woman I silently re-named Little Crane because at times the vessel of disgust just spills over. Without justice for Nita Estevez, she would be three times abandoned: first to poverty, then to death, last to memory.

I wanted her killer because, under the merciless green tint of fluorescent lights as she lay in the cool chamber of the dead, we had come to learn she had been *alive* when she was beaten, throttled, raped, and had her nipple bitten off.

14

CHAPTER 2

A week later we had no more meaningful evidence than the day we walked out of the murder scene.

I had worked that case and several others all week and had gone four days before that without a day off. I thought I had Sunday finally, and planned to meet my pal, Ray Vega, in San Juan Capistrano for the Swallow's Day Parade. Then Stu Hollings, my supervisor, called at six A.M. and asked me to cover a scene in an area of the city of Irvine named Technology Park where computer geeks toil. "Remember," he said, "victims don't get a day off." I could argue the point but didn't.

Irvine is a vast, flat, master-planned and virtually aseptic city so dirt-free you could drop a sandwich, pick it up, and eat it without a thought. A breeze could blow between buildings of the business park where the body was found and not lift a single leaf. It was not a place you might imagine a man to be sitting against a white wall with a bullet drilled through his head.

I found the slug bored into the stucco behind him, and stood by while the coroner's investigator taped bags over the victim's hands so fingernail scrapings could be taken at the morgue. The scene was shut down in under three hours with precious little to show for it. But the man did have ID; plenty of it. He was supposed to be 21 years old. With the damage of death, it was hard to hazard a guess. On his employee badge and driver's license he was Hector Victor Flores. The name on an old Border Crosser card forbidding work in the U.S. was Hector Ramon Gonzales. And the name on a fake Resident Alien card, known as a "green card" although it is actually pink, was Hector Joaquin René Martinez. I examined that one carefully because I knew something was not quite right about it, then realized it bore a full-face photo instead of the required one showing an ear.

As I took my small collection of evidence to Property at the lab, I was thinking that the young man should be just now stirring in a bedroom on this day of rest, or reading a Spanish version of the Sunday paper to find a new used car, or chomping on a cold tortilla stuffed with leftovers while he figured out which movie or air show to attend. Where he shouldn't be, was lying on a steel gurney at the morgue.

"Having a good *T-I-M-E?*"

The giant bird bobbed toward me and Ray Vega, gold beak flapping. We stood beneath a huge sycamore tree along the parade route. The celebration was to mark the day the tiny gunmetal-blue birds known as barn swallows return from their winter retreat. They would build mud cups beneath town eaves and mission arches while issuing soft *vit-vits, slip-lips,* and long musical twitters. But this big-footed, ugly, slightly frightening, man-sized swallow stirred edgy giggles as he advanced on spectators. He whirled, drew his six-shooter, and plugged a cow-dude sneaking up on him smack dead in the street. The crowd shrieked, laughed, then applauded.

I looked down the line of parade watchers. Most were Anglos but many bore the dark hair and tawny skin of Hispanic/Indian mix like Ray, by my side, and the victim who only hours ago leaned against a building in what now seemed another world.

"Damn it," Ray said, "I want to see some swallows floculating."

I said, "Your mouth, son."

16

"No, really. They swoop, they dive, they get it *on*."

"Me, I'm mad I missed the Hairiest Man Contest," I said. At that, Ray milked his chin, feeling for a beard. "Forget it, sweetie," I said, "they had two months' head start."

The jumbo swallow was headed for our side again. I told Ray the bird's beak was the wrong color. Let him know, Ray said. So I did, amateur birder that I am. "Your bill should be yellow," I called, and immediately regretted it.

The giant swallow froze and glared at me, folded a wing onto his hip, and said, "I beg your *P-A-R-DON?!*" He touched his holster. I shrank back, and with that the critter was well appeased, for he whirled again and went for a troop of small Indians alongside a rickety covered wagon with the word "BUCKAROOS" painted on the canvas, but not before flipping his long, dragging, split tail at us.

"Mooned by a swallow," I said.

"I hate a parade," said Ray. He was out of his usual beige-and-khaki California Highway Patrol uniform, wearing instead the outfit of the Fiesta Posse: white shirt, black hat, jeans, and boots, and a bolo cinched by a blob of turquoise. If he were of a mind today, he'd haul off any man found clean-shaven or any outlaw of either sex found drinking nonalcoholic beverages or not wearing Western attire. They'd be thrown in the hoosegow—*husgado*, Ray called it—till they could pay their dollar fines and be set free.

But by the look of it, Ray would do no more than tip his hat to the ladies and be the handsome cop-dude he was. Ray is funny, naughty, sexy and single, my friend and only my friend, though sometimes there's a lot of flirting going on. Not to flirt, to Ray, is not to breathe. "Where's Sanders?" he said. "He owes me a beer."

"Joe's bringing his son," I said. "I'm a little nervous. 'The other woman' thing."

"You're not the other woman."

"His parents break up after twenty-three years of marriage and then there's this, this—"

"—babe," Ray offered.

"—in his dad's life."

"You know it wasn't that way."

"Does that help a kid deal with it?" I said. "I don't know."

Behind the buckaroos came a pitiful-sounding junior high school band, the girls with flat chests and orange legs from choosing the wrong shade of panty hose. Close on their heels a herd of dogs in cowboy scarves towed volunteers from the animal shelter by leashes.

Ray said, "What's David now, twenty? He's way more interested in his own next piece of ass than his father's."

"Thanks for framing it so delicately." Ray formed his middle finger into a circle with his thumb and moved it toward me as if to flick me on side of the head. "Watch it," I said.

"I could give a dink about the rest of this," he said. "Where's those Soiled Doves they promised?" He let his gaze follow a woman astride an ebony horse whose hair matched her horse's color. She was dressed in a turn-of-the-century green velvet dress. The gleaming strands of the mount's tail spilled to the blacktop, then broke for another six inches like dark water over a fall. For a reason I didn't know I flashed on the scene with Nita Estevez in the Santa Ana hovel.

When Ray hiked up on a low stone wall and sat there banging his boots against the rock, I joined him. "I almost didn't make it today. I had a callout this morning in Irvine, off Alton. Single round to the head."

"Gang stuff? I'm tellin' ya, we should build a camp. Shut down San Onofre Nuclear Plant, put all the wetbacks down there cleanin' it up, no spacesuits to wear. Fry their *frijoles*."

"How can you say that? Your ancestors were from over the border."

"*My* ancestors didn't have any border—*comprende?* You guys stole *California* and *made up* a border."

"Get over it," I said.

He rubbed his hand over my back. "Mm. No bra."

"Come on. Let's see if Joe's here yet," I said. We threaded through the crowd, which thickened near makeshift *mercados* displaying souvenirs, and made our way to the front of a saloon called The Swallow's Inn. Men and women stood jammed in the doorway holding beers. The women wore lacy garter belts over their jeans and the men sported giant brass sheriff's badges and hats slid high on their foreheads.

Ray said he'd forge one way looking for Joe and I could take the other. A woman squeezed by Ray with an appreciative look. She wore a shirt printed like the Classified ads, one circled in red: "Cowboy Wanted."

I detoured to the room where the band was playing for all it was worth and dancers had about a foot to move in. Glued to the ceiling were tin buckets, tractor seats, boots, ballet slippers, and a naked, chubby toy doll with a cigarette dangling from her rosebud lips. I didn't see Joe and came back up to the main room, then spied him in a line by the restrooms. He was with his son. David looked like him. Taller, maybe six feet, but his blue eyes were Joe's and his hair was a mass of dark curls already shot with silver. He wore white jeans and a brick-colored Western shirt to his dad's blue denim. David shook my hand, and if there was anything readable in his eyes having to do with me being his dad's girlfriend, I missed it.

Ray came up on the side, and Joe introduced him too. "Don't mess with these two," Joe said. "They'll pop you for ripping labels off pillows." Ray was eye-flirting with every woman within ten feet.

I asked if I should order them something while they were standing in line. Joe cut his hand across his eyebrows, full to there, while David shook his head no. "Okay, see you in a minute," I said, and headed for the bar just as a woman tapped Ray on the elbow and nodded toward the dance floor. Next time I looked, the two were scrunched among the born to boogie, making moves to "Teach Your Children" by the Red Hots. I snagged a beer, then worked my way outside.

The courtyard in back contained a jacaranda tree in purple bud, surrounded by a wrought-iron bench with no one on it. I grabbed it and watched smoke from a wagon-type grill off to the side ascend into the air as a hefty man in an apron turned patties.

When I looked back at the doorway, Joe's son was framed there. A woman in a shirt that said "Bite Me" noticed him too. David stepped down and came and sat on the bench alongside me, leaning forward with a hand at the end of one knee.

"So what do you think?" I said.

"About what?"

"This shindig."

He shrugged, then straightened and leaned back.

"Your dad tells me you're attending U.C. Irvine," I said.

He nodded.

"How's it going? You like it?"

Two nods is what I got for an answer this time. I took a stick of gum out of my shirt pocket and offered him one. He took it, then neatly re-folded the foil wrapper to tuck it back into the outer one the way his father did. I wondered why he came to sit by me at all and decided to be quiet and let what would emerge, emerge. Finally he said, "This isn't about you."

I said: "I'm sorry?"

"You work with my dad, right?"

"Right."

"You see a lot of things."

"You could say so."

"Let me ask you something."

"Go ahead."

The tip of his boot jostled a clutch of gray sow bugs in the grass between the patio bricks. The smallest tanks tucked into themselves like beads; the biggest tried to lumber away. David deliberately blocked it until it, too, curled shut. Then he pulled in his legs and leaned forward, not making eye contact with me. His voice was low and weighted when he said, "Did you ever find yourself having to . . . like, roll over on somebody?"

"I'm not sure what you're getting at."

"Roll over on someone. Rat someone out."

I paused a moment. "It's not something I usually think about on our side of the line. Why?" He just met me. Why wasn't he talking to his dad if he had something on his mind?

Ray appeared in the back door holding a beer, scanning the area till he saw us. I raised a hand behind David's back to signal "Stop," and he nodded and stepped back in.

"Your dad loves you a lot, you know," I said.

David stood. "Is there a phone around somewhere?"

"We can go find out."

"No, that's okay."

I'd lost him. "Wait," I said. "I think I know where one might be." We went out onto the sidewalk, where a woman in traditional Spanish costume with flowing skirts and *mantilla* led three little girls in similar dress ahead of us until we crossed the street. We headed for a restaurant converted from a railroad freight car, where I waited on the wooden platform while David went in. From a tree limb above me, a brown towhee in his creamy bib and dark necklace made sounds like a coin falling into a pot.

The boards under me moved and I heard a deep sigh and knew it was David. "All set?" I asked. He gave a quick nod but didn't move. "Want to walk? You could buy your girlfriend an Indian necklace or something."

"I don't feel like looking at things."

We headed for the shade of the sycamore Ray and I had stood under a while ago, only now we were a level above the street. There, we sat at an old picnic table at the edge of a vocational school. Signatures, dates, gang signs, and obscenities were cut into the tabletop. David pulled a twig from a crack in the table and began scoring its bark with a thumbnail. "Question," he said.

"Fire away."

"You've got a friend. . . ."

"One or two."

"This person's real smart. He's twenty-six and already has half a mil in the bank."

"Sounds like a good friend to have."

"Maybe this friend—hypothetically, now . . ."

"Sure."

"Say he's into something he shouldn't be. Like, illegal."

"Would that be drugs?" I thought he was clamming up again, but then he said no. "This thing. Would it be threatening to *you?*" Behind him, a boy crossing the playing field balanced a soccer ball on his upturned fingers.

David flicked the twig away. "That's not exactly it."

"Have you confronted him?"

"It's not like that. I can't . . . bring it up to him. It's complicated."

"Is there someone on campus you can talk to?"

Now his eyes searched mine as if finding something dif-

ferent in each one. He looked so forlorn I wanted to reach out
my hand and touch him on a shoulder, but I grew timid. He
got up and moved to the tree and stood there, the back of his
shirt forming a rusty wedge down to his waist. I went to stand
next to him. Below, the parade crowd had thinned. "Whatever it is that's troubling you, David, I think you should tell
your dad."

"Don't say anything to him, please," he said urgently.

"There's nothing to tell, now is there?"

"Just don't say anything."

"I won't. But eventually it's best to get it out in the air."

Hanging his thumbs in his back pockets, he kicked at a
gray tree root risen from the ground in search of water so that
it bore the height and shape of a concrete bumper. Below on
the street two blondes and two cops stood at the end of the
parade line talking. The women wore black leather jackets
and fringy denim shorts, their long legs ending in boots. I
thought David was looking at them too, when I heard him
say, "He's here!"

"Who?" His face had gone slack. "Your dad?"

Abruptly, he turned and took a few steps away toward the
playing field, where the grass was still yellow from Southern
California's brand of winter. The sky was the clear blue you
see in magazines, and piled with white clouds.

He recovered and said, "No, not my dad. Listen, it's theft,
okay? My roommate's stealing stuff. I thought I saw him
down there just now. But it couldn't be him." His laugh bore
a shading of scorn. "He wouldn't be caught dead at something like this."

"Stealing stuff? Property, money, what?"

David shook his head as if he were stupid or the whole universe was.

"Can you prove it," I said, "what he's doing?"

"Rat out your friends and you're just a different species of rat."

"Not always," I said.

"So-called 'situational ethics,' right? I took a philosophy class once. Some things are not so wrong *if*, right? But I can't buy into it. You just don't tattle."

"Well, then, I guess we've pretty well covered it," I said. Something more than a moral stubbornness played here, but I didn't have a clue as to what, or why he would disclose this stuff to me, a virtual stranger, and frankly I was a little annoyed at this boy I didn't know, and hungry for a beer.

Across the street when we reached the sidewalk, a white terrier in a front window of a house stood on the back of a couch and barked wildly.

In second grade, I watched a friend slip her hand in the pocket of a green coat belonging to another child while all the other kids were at the tables making Play-Doh animals. Her fist was closed when it came out, and when she opened it, her palm held a silver dollar. She saw me, but neither of us said anything, not then, not later; not to the teacher nor to the little girl who owned the coat and who was crying at the bus stop when I walked by that afternoon. I hated myself for not doing what I should have: gone up to the offender and told her to give the coin back. Instead, I avoided my friend who'd turned thief before my eyes until avoiding her became part of the crime itself, and it niggled at me after all these years.

We were nearing the street to turn on to reach the Swallow Inn when David said, "Thanks for trying."

"Somehow I think you'll find the right thing to do," I said.

He smiled a little and said, "Dad says all I have under my hat is hair." We walked by a silver Jaguar parked at an angle, taking up two parking spaces. Dave said, "Overpriced bucket of bolts."

"You couldn't tell it by me."

He said, "Ever back up over gate prongs?"

"Not that I remember."

"I did that."

"For fun, or what?"

"I forgot a book at school, backed up before I thought," he said, shaking his head. "It'll be fun all right, paying Dad off."

"I'm really sorry," I said, but had to smile.

In the street in front of the mission, line-dancers were doing the Texas Swing to "Bad Moon A-Risin' " blasting from enormous P.A. speakers.

The saloon was still packed with people shouting over dozens of others. We found Joe and Ray in a corner with a couple of cops and a sunburned brunette in a little bitty blouse, the bunch of them red-eyed and having the good time they should on an off-duty day.

I decided to head home and let them call me a party-poop if they would. And they did. But I kissed both Ray and Joe on the cheek, nodded to the brunette and the deputies, and shook hands with David, telling him to take care. He held on a fraction more than he needed, it seemed, and again I felt I'd lost somehow but didn't know exactly why.

On my way out, a man in a white cowboy hat who looked East-Indian asked me if I knew the two-step. "Next time, Duke," I said, and squeezed through the doorway.

It took me a minute to get through the crowd and around the building, and when I did I saw Dave Sanders outside again in the courtyard, alone, sitting on the same bench we sat on earlier, with his head bent to his hand as if he had a headache that just would not let go.

CHAPTER 3

On the way home from the parade I stopped at a car wash, got the jiffy job, and watched a limping Hispanic man with white sideburns slap rags on car roofs and wipe milkshake off consoles and road-tar off wheel covers.

I thought of the victim in Technology Park, of healthy size and youthful years. Who would miss him? What woman did not yet know he was gone? I thought about the endless chain of grief until I tired of thinking about it and walked over and got a drink of water and read the bulletin board.

It was almost five when I got home and climbed the outside stairs to my condo overlooking Newport Bay. The sun was painting the bluffs gold, while the water lay black and still as an oil spill.

My guinea pig in the laundry room whistled for attention. "Just a minute, baby," I called. The phone was ringing too.

Joe was on the line. "So what'd you think? He's a hunk, wouldn't you say?" His voice carried post-parade effects.

"Definitely starter material," I said.

"Damn tootin'. Takes after his dad."

"You're going to feel terrible in the morning."

"Hey, doll, how'd you like to meet me at The Quiet Woman?"

"That might be good."

At that, he said, "I'm thinking of taking some vacation."

"Did I hear right? If you cashed in *all* your accumulated days you could take off permanently."

"Take tomorrow off with me."

"I've got half a dozen cases I should be working on," I said. "The Doe this morning doesn't help any."

"What'd you tell me about that, again?"

"Later. I've got to feed my guinea pig. If you can, amidst all that fun you'll be having, call me tomorrow."

"Okay. Goodnight, Tomorrow."

Stu had left a message on my desk to come see him first thing. We had another unidentified gunshot victim.

"Find us something on this one, Brandon," he said, looking up over his glasses from his desk. "Two Doe's, two days. Not good. And I don't want to hear 'I'll do my best.' Best isn't good enough. Find something."

I didn't mind working for Stu, but he'd been an administrator too long. At 6 A.M. his shirtsleeves were already rolled. His desktop was a picture of perfect geometry, papers stacked squarely, pencils parallel.

"Homicide on this is Boyd Russell. Maybe I'll send Sanders out. You want Joe? I'll see if he's free." He reached for the phone.

"Joe's taking a vacation day." Stu gave me a look as if that were impossible. Stu, about Joe's age, pegged me as still a rookie though I'd been in the lab seven years and had logged two earlier in uniform in Oakland. "I'm thinking about a day off myself, maybe Friday?"

"Is it necessary?"

"Stu, I've had one day off in eleven."

" 'Can't stand the heat' . . ." he said.

"Isn't there a policy on that, so many days in a row?"

"For women. You want to call that in?"

"No."

"Bring me something on this Doe and we'll see."

"Stu, you're all heart," I said. He believed I meant it.

The higher I drove, the bigger the mansions became.

Nellie Gail is a hilly subdivision in the city of Laguna Hills, a few miles south of Irvine. Homes there run worthy of a Kennedy clan. Streets are not streets but "parkways" and "avenidas;" they intersect with rounded corners. Backyards spill in long slopes and in them are classy swimming pools and rows of fruit trees and corrals draped with bougainvillea in blazing salmon, pink, and magenta. The horses wear crisp green fly-masks as they munch from grain buckets and flick their wiry tails. Goats stand stiff-legged, chickens pose on boulders, and black sheep swing their lower jaws nonchalantly over fresh alfalfa spears. Another world here than the one in downtown Santa Ana, central county; another world entirely.

I pulled up to Gallup Circle across from a park. It was misty, no sun out today, promoting the smell of camphor from the many eucalyptus trees. Carnival trees, Ray Vega calls them. "Carnival trees," he says: "U-clipped-us." Three nannies, in colored sweaters over white uniforms tending children on the playset, turned their honey-gold faces to me as I got out of the car.

Two black-and-white sheriff's units were parked under the U-clipped-us, while a third was at the far end of a line of yellow scene tape strung across the trunks of several trees.

I walked up to one of the deputies, a man I knew from a case a year ago that took us to long waits in court hallways and what-a-tough-job-it-is conversations. "Hi, Art. I hear we have a homicide bright and early."

"I'm thinking suicide," he said, and pointed up the hill.

"What does Homicide say?"

"Not here yet. Stuck in traffic." He hiked his belt laden

with gear, and went on: "I checked the weapon. Little peashooter."

"Okay," I said.

"Okay? Okay? I don't get any rise out of ya?"

"Can I yell at you later?"

"I had to clear the weapon, Smokey, you know that."

"Two rounds out of seven," Art said, and pointed under his chin. "Poor dumb shit had to shoot himself twice. Time comes *I'm* thinking serious suicide, I'm damn sure usin' a bigger gun."

"It's not the bullet that kills ya, it's the hole," I said.

"I still don't see how a guy could cap himself twice," another deputy said.

"People do the damnedest things, ain't that right, Smokey?"

"That they do."

Long ago, I'd read a book on suicide by one of the Doctors Meninger of the famous clinic. Curdled my blood, you could say.

"No casings around though," Art said, "is what has me bothered. Maybe you can find them. Also, looks like a California collie's been gnawin' on his foot. Bigger 'n life, I see this ol' dude come right down off the hill and go loping across the park." When he pointed, the nannies, whose faces had been trained in our direction, quickly glanced away. "I almost took a shot at him."

"Contrary to rumors, Art, you're a bright man."

"A guy with a shotgun in the closet and a three-year-old in the back yard will blast the hell out of that thing one of these days. I would, I lived here."

When I started for the hill, the other deputy said, "Better wait for Homicide." I gave him a look, said nothing, then waded through a carpet of lavender Mexican poppies at the foot of the slope.

The victim sat against the trunk of a tree, head sagged forward. One ankle was marred with purple bands. I knew at once the marks were not from a coyote. The animal would've gone for the bigger wound, first to lick the drainage and then to topple the body over for an easier feast.

In the right hand lay a .25 semi-auto. Its magazine lay on top of a brown paper sack where Arty had put it, blocked from sliding down the slope by a patch of weed. A few feet back I located a flat spot on which to set my kit and camera. I drew a map, then took a number of shots, and finally pulled on latex gloves. I wanted to see the hole, the hole that kills ya.

Ordinarily, nobody touches the body until the coroner's people do, but there are exceptions. L.A.'s not Orange County, Orange County's not Fresno, Chicago's not New York, and none of it is Kermit, Texas. There's a lot more latitude at crime scenes than people know.

The back of the victim's jacket collar was a tarry red. Ants ran a two-lane course on the tree behind, business as usual. I took hold of the victim's hair and lifted the head to check for the onset of rigor. It gave, with only slight resistance. Blood that had pooled in the mouth drooled out.

Entry, as Art had said, was under the chin, with sooting at one edge of the hole, indicating a near-contact wound. The size of the hole looked bigger to me than that from a .25, but I wasn't a pathologist and maybe two rounds would do that. On the other hand, it didn't seem likely a person could put two in a single channel, no matter that I'd read about and seen some strange things. Art thought there were two rounds because it was a seven-round magazine and two were missing, but maybe he didn't have it loaded to capacity, or maybe he fired a trial round as he worked up courage. No brass around to prove it, though it could have rolled downhill.

I lowered the head and examined the exit wound. It also seemed larger to me than what a .25-caliber might inflict, but again, I was not a coroner's assistant, I was an evidence junkie.

Bending over to look at the gun, I didn't see anything that might be blowback on it, bits of blood and tissue, though microscoped at the lab, it might show. Once again I raised the head to look at a face that might not have made it out of the teens. In his eyebrows and on his cheeks were flecks of dirt, as if he'd rested or been thrown upon the ground. Beard growth was uneven. The eyes were half-open and had lost their sheen.

I whispered, "Who did this to you, fella?"

I released his head forward. That the head gave at all could mean he'd met his death within the last four hours, since rigor both begins and ends first in the small muscles of the head and extremities. Several things can affect rigor: activity before death, ambient temperature, drug use. In rare cases, rigor never asserts itself, as in some very obese or very small people. By eighteen hours rigor is in retreat; the body becomes flaccid again. I didn't think the victim had been up here, in this wealthy neighborhood, undiscovered that long.

When I applied pressure on the bluish-red coloring on the side of his palm, there was a blanching. The color signified a condition called postmortem lividity, or *livor mortis,* which occurs when gravity pools the blood in the capillaries to the lowest body portions. I removed a glove and touched the skin: cool as a mannequin. Body temp, or *algor mortis,* would be taken at the morgue and matched with time charts to aid in what must remain, without a witness to the crime, only an estimate for time of death.

I glanced downhill and saw the feet of several civilians through the veil of tree limbs, and hands connected to leashes with dogs on the other end. Somewhere the raucous sound of leaf blowers began. Then I saw the coroner's van and a beige car pull up. Boyd Russell had made it.

I was taking swabs from the stain on the tree when he came up. Long of face, high of forehead, with gray bags beneath his eyes, Boyd was wearing a tan suit and a shirt that already looked rumpled. He looked like a million middle-aged men in any profession, one who probably paid his taxes on the last eligible day, went to church for the sake of the kids, and watched ball games on t.v. and re-runs of "Hunter."

I reported what I'd done so far. He asked if anyone had checked the higher part of the hill above us, where two massive, cream-colored water tanks surrounded by a chain-link fence hunkered behind a hedge. "Not that I know of," I said.

"Go take a look around, will you? Let me get the lay of this here and I'll join you in a minute."

I looped my camera cord around my neck, gathered several small brown evidence sacks from my kit, and walked at an angle up the slope, plowing through a spill of gold gazanias, their long-fingered petals folded skyward as if praying for sun.

As I walked the fence around the water tank, I saw a cigarette butt, a piece of cellophane, a beer can—kids out smoking and drinking in the bushes, maybe. Not exactly what you'd call evidence, but I set position markers, shot some frames, and bagged the items anyway, numbering the sacks and applying labels over the folds, and writing down identifying info in my notes as well. Some forensics jocks say it's possible to take too many notes, that they can get you in trouble, trip you up in court, but I haven't found it that way. Later Boyd would ring doorbells to ask neighbors if they saw anything; if they had teenage kids who might've seen anything; if they had teenage kids who may have sneaked off to

suck a few brews on the sly and leave their litter on the landscape, and if so, these items could be eliminated as part of the
case.

The gate to the first water tank was padlocked. I moved on
to the second one, which also had a gate but was free of a lock.
Inside the lower walkway I found the ladder that allowed
access to the top. I left the sealed bags on the ground and
draped my jacket over the wire fence. Then, with a jump, I
caught a rung and climbed. When the ladder became raised
handholds on the curved dome, I stood and walked to the
center. In the foggy distance a pack of low hills floated like
whales in a white ocean.

The raw call of a crow ripped overhead; leaves rustled. I
saw his hard eyes and the shine of his jointed feet as the
branch swelled up and down with his weight. Then he lifted
off, to perch over the second water tank. Only then did I spy
the brown tent of a wallet standing against the last handhold
on the second tank's dome. Not far from it, draped over an air
valve, lay what looked like a silver chain and medallion.

"Damn," I muttered. Maybe I was going to have something to make old Stu happy after all.

"It could be nothing," I told Boyd Russell when I got
down. "But there's a lock on the gate and the cage at the
bottom of the ladder."

"We'll fix that," he said. We both went to his car. He got a
bolt cutter out of the trunk, and when I saw a wire coat hanger
in the dark recess by the wheel well, I asked for that too.

Boyd cut the locks. I climbed the tank with my camera,
sacks, and the straightened coat hanger to retrieve the wallet
and medallion. Down again, I put on fresh gloves and opened
the wallet. Inside were grocery store coupons of the sort the
checker hands you with your receipt, and another poorly
counterfeited green card. It wouldn't have fooled a drunk

man in a dark alley. The photo did seem to be of the victim but it was clearly glued on and I knew the Alien Number was about four digits short. The name on the card was Hector Bonifacio Rios. Another Hector. The birthdate made him twenty-four.

A folded snapshot in the back pocket showed people at a party. Three Hispanic men and women with bright smiles on their faces. One of the women stood behind the far end of the couch with her arm around a man and her face pressed into his sweater. I recognized him as the dead man on the hill. Smiling. Handsome. Young. Alive. I wanted to will him back, as if you could run life's film in reverse.

After the coroner's investigator took tape-lifts of the debris on the victim's face and applied them to 3x5 cards, she had her two attendants pack up the body and remove it. I snapped a few more shots and searched the ground beneath. With an army knife I poked around in the tree bark until I felt a solid stoppage, and dug out a slug, a single slug. I stashed it in a small black film canister after showing it to Boyd.

"Looks to be maybe a thirty-eight," he said.

"That's about how I'd call it," I said.

Boyd said. "Get the ballistics. I bet it won't match the gun over there. Just doesn't look small enough."

I stayed a while longer, checking the area again and even asking the deputies to lift their shoes to see if any brass had lodged in the ridges of their soles. But the simple fact is you can't count on much for evidence in outdoor scenes. You can go after spent shell casings, dropped weapons, blood stains, witnesses, and victim ID. You can take fingerprints off trees, but unlikely. You can take them off toilet paper in a toilet, the insides of gloves, the sticky side of tape, off concrete sidewalks, even the victim's skin, though none of these is without its own set of difficulties.

Find something, Stu had said. Okay. I did. Two dead Hispanics in the space of two days, both with gunshot wounds to the head, both in outdoor scenes. Fake ID's with the given name "Hector."

But if that added up to anything, it was as elusive as a shadow sped across the moon.

CHAPTER 4

I stopped at Del Taco for an early lunch and sat in my car and
threw bits of tortilla from a burrito to a Brewer's blackbird and
three wrens.

Music crackled from an outside speaker, Gloria Estefan
singing "It's Too Late." The DJ came on and said we were in
for a perfect 72 degrees. I wondered how Joe was spending his
rare vacation day, hoped he was poolside with a drink, a
book, and soft music, or barefoot on the beach, watching
pretty girls go by.

When I got to the lab, a colleague named Jerry was leaving out
the back door, grumbling about AFIS, the automated fingerprint
system, being down. I could still log in the evidence from the
Nellie Gail scene, prepare fingerprint cards, and examine the
tape lifts holding the leaf debris. I passed by Joe's office on the
way to my desk and there he was, sitting there big as life.

"Liar," I said from his doorway.

"What can I say? I love my job." A few years before I met
him he'd had a heart attack. He could easily take light duty if
he wanted, but he didn't and this was an example.

I sat in the chair in front of his desk and said, "Can't you
even give yourself one day? One single day?"

"When David's classes are over we're going rafting on the
Kern River. Then you'll be complaining, 'Where's Joe?'"

I dug out a small pack of M&Ms and fished a finger in.
"Want some?" Joe shook his head and made a slight face.
"That tequila will getcha every time," I said.

"It's not a hangover."

"Sorry to tell you, but it's called a hangover."

"We still on for tonight?" he asked. "How's six?"

"Fine."

"Heard you had one out at Nellie Gail this morning."

"Correct. We have ID, but it seems hokey."

"GSW?" Joe asked.

"Here," I said and touched the point under my chin where the victim sustained the gunshot wound. "Two rounds. No casings. He had a twenty-five caliber in his hand, but I took a slug out of a tree behind him that looks bigger, but it's hard to know for sure until Firearms sees it."

"Ear witnesses?"

"None so far." On his desk I saw a familiar case file. "Something new on your Dana Point case?"

"Not really."

Six weeks ago Joe attended a scene where a woman's body was discovered on a high ocean bluff after her small dog returned to their neighbor's house dragging its leash. The husband, when he was told, was too nonchalant, playing a radio strapped to his belt the whole time of the interview. He answered questions without rancor and seemed to cooperate, but Joe thought the guy was guilty as hell and every once in a while hauled out the case file.

He stood and rounded the desk and said, "Come out to the car with me. I have a present for you." He stopped when I didn't trail him. "Why the face? I just felt like giving you a present."

"You know they make me feel . . ."

"Funny," he said.

"Gifts are like pants before the advent of suspenders," I said. "They're too hard to keep up."

"How long have you been planning to use that one?"

"Long time," I said.

In the parking lot, a bird hurtled onto a low limb of a jacaranda tree whose purple buds were partially open. Joe said, "Name that bird."

"That's an LBJ." He waited for me elaborate. "Little Brown Job," I said.

"For that," Joe said, "you don't get your present till tonight," and pocketed his keys. Then, looking beyond me, he said, "What happened to your car? That's your ride over there, isn't it?"

We went over to my car, backed into the slot. My heart sank. All along the passenger side was a deep scratch. Joe bent down to inspect it. "That's not from somebody parking too close. Where you been hanging out?"

"Nowhere. Well, with *you* and bad company like Ray Vega."

"There you have it," he said, teasing.

Back inside, I had two phone messages waiting. I was on the second return call when my boss dropped by and stood in the doorway. I wasn't able to get off the phone right away. He left. When I got off that call, I phoned the morgue to find out the autopsy schedule for the Doe's so I'd have something to tell Stu. They were backed up. It probably wouldn't be till Thursday.

The rest of the afternoon I worked on the Nellie Gail and never saw Stu and never saw Joe again before I left. When I went to my car and got reminded of its damage, I wasn't even mad anymore, just resigned.

The crowd at The Quiet Woman was noisy from a birthday party, the honoree screaming her surprise at every turn. Joe and I hid in a booth, wishing the establishment's name applied. The wooden sign near the front door was a painted depiction of a woman in Dutch dress, minus a head;

hence, the quiet woman. Legend has it she incurred the fatal wrath of her relatives by talking too much.

Over the racket, Joe mentioned again that something seemed to be bothering his son.

I sipped my wine and asked benignly, "Girl trouble?"

"Don't think so. And as far as I know, he's doing okay in school. So says Jennifer. She usually gets something out of him."

Behind us the birthday girl was opening a pink package, crying, "Amy-y-y, you *shouldn't*."

Joe said, "It's like he can't finish a thought, a sentence. His knees bounce. We'll be sitting somewhere, his knee takes on a life of its own. He'll put his own hand on it. Then the other one starts."

I felt guilty for not telling Joe what his son said about his roommate. But a confidence is a confidence, and that's that.

"I mean, we already had the sex talk, what, five years ago," Joe said. He took my hand and said, "Do something to your hair?"

"Washed it." I gave him a nuzzle.

"How novel," he said. The curve of lines by his deep-socket eyes and the rich smell of his skin set me to amorous thoughts.

When I clicked back in, Joe was saying, "He's busy enough. He's into a game called *Go*. Chinese. You play with little stones. I've never seen it. Besides that, he's doing this conservation project near Culver and Michelson, in there. So it *seems* like everything's going all right."

"David will be fine. He probably wants to hit you up for a loan for his gambling debts."

"He owes me for tires."

I smiled. "He told me about that."

"He did, huh? Was I ever that dumb, I wonder?"

"Probably."

The server brought our meals: halibut and halibut.

"Tell me," I asked Joe, "what do you know about Boyd Russell? He's the investigator on my two Doe's."

"Russell? He's okay. Nothing exactly faulty. Just no imagination, no creativity." He looked down at his drink. I had the feeling there was more he wasn't telling me.

"What else?"

He paused, then said, "The way he conducts his private life." He regarded me with half-closed eyes. "Has Boyd hit on you yet?"

"*Boyd?* No," I said, laughing.

"Watch him next time you're on an investigation with him. He spends a lot more time interviewing the women than the men."

I slipped along the leather booth, closing the space. "Yeah? How about losing this joint, you and me? You been hit on, buddy."

The moon rode low on the bluffs near the bay as we drove. Joe had a CD of Carly Simon's "Boys in the Trees" playing, a favorite of mine. When we reached my place he hauled out a package wrapped in red tissue paper, twisted off with a red curly ribbon. He brought it into the house and set it on the coffee table, then took a seat on the sofa.

I unwrapped it, exposing a stuffed Tasmanian Devil dressed in a leather biker jacket and a red bandanna. "Remind you of anyone?" Joe asked. It did: a certain biker of the felon variety: One Monty Blackman from a case two years earlier, Harley rider, bar owner, pig farmer, smuggler, general all 'round rough trade.

When I looked at Joe, he had a hand on his stomach again.

40

"Are you all right?"

"Water would be good."

On my way to the kitchen I put on music I bought because I knew Joe would like it: Linda Ronstadt, songs of the Forties. Joe was on the balcony looking over the bay when I came back. The inky bay was glossed with the cast light of local businesses along the coast. He stepped back in and sat at the counter and said, "C'mere," tapping his leg.

I did, and put my arms around his neck and whispered, "Thanks for Taz."

"Don't mention it, lady." He gave me a kiss, and just as it was getting interesting, he said, "You know, babe, I think I should call it a night."

"Already? You want a Tums or something?"

"I think I'll just go on home."

"Tomorrow night, then."

He paused, then said softly, "Hey, kid. You're not neglecting your other friends for this old man, are you?"

"In the first place," I said, "I don't know any old men. And in the second, no." I got off his lap but stood close.

His palm ran up and down my leg. "You know if you ever want to date someone else, it's all right, don't you?"

I gave the leg of his stool a kick.

He said, "Just making sure we covered that ground."

"We have. Before."

"Just so you know you're a free agent."

"What about Boyd Russell?"

"You want to date *him?*"

"I'm *say*ing, you don't like it that *he* sleeps around."

"He's married. That's the difference. I only want the best for you," he said.

"Then you're wishing for what I already have."

He got up to go. "We have that wedding Saturday."

"Right," I said. "Sunday I'm going on an Audubon cleanup. To help clear out invasive plants down along San Juan Creek. That'll kill the morning, but you want to do something later?"

"Boy, you sure plan far ahead."

"It's because I haven't had a weekend in so long it seems like a vacation."

At the door Joe said, "I'm supposed to go look at cars with David Sunday. He's trading up. Old Dad here may have to be making the payments even though Dave says he got a raise at the bookstore. Did I tell you he's working in the college bookstore? Stacking books."

"Right."

"I asked him if he was reading any. He says sure. Then he tells me a joke he read in one, which was not exactly what I had in mind."

"You going to keep it to yourself?"

"Hm?"

"The joke."

"It's an Aggie joke. Texas Agricultural. Nerd-U," he said. "So this Aggie was trying to light a match. The first one doesn't work. He throws it away, tries another. That one doesn't light either. Throws it away. Strikes a third. Poof! It fires. He blows it out, says, 'That's a good one. I gotta save it!' "

"Oh moan."

"You asked."

I stood on the front balcony and watched him go to his car. A corner floodlight gave luster to his silver hair, and his brown leather jacket shone like rich mud as he walked and juggled his keys hand-to-hand.

CHAPTER 5

I had a training class the next morning at nine that had been set up six weeks before. There'd still be enough time to meet Ray Vega for a little pre-work plinking at a range that lets cops come in early. On the way, my cell phone rang.

"Smokey, Ray," he said.

"How'd I know it would be you?"

"I can't make it this morning."

"You jerk," I said.

His voice gravelly, he said, "You never had a hard night?"

"Plenty of 'em, but I don't stand up my friends. You're gettin' old, Ray-boy."

"On that you may be right," he said. "What the hell am I? Thirty-one, Jesus. I gotta snag some sleep. Hey, you ever get that gun you were going to?" I pictured him sitting on the side of his bed in his shorts, head in his hand, phone clamped to his ear.

"Yeah, I bought it. Five-shot snubby. What's it to ya? You can't get your ass out of bed to come see."

He sighed or yawned again, and said, "That hurts."

"Cry me a river."

"I'm thinking of getting me a new backup," he said. "What kind'd you say?"

"I already told you."

"I mean, what *kind*."

"Smith Airweight. Spurless."

"Like it?"

"Gun's great. Shooter's terrible." He yawned again in my

43

ear. "Go back to bed, Raymond."

"Nah, I gotta get up. Hey, Smokey?"

"What?"

"You should see this new girl. . . ."

"Oh no, Raymond. Not another one."

"You have to meet her. She's special."

"They're all special, Ray. You notice a pattern there?" A slow sedan listing to one side pulled ahead of me, causing me to change lanes. "Two cars on a long run of nothin', and this guy has to pull in front of me. Where are you when I need you?"

"Shoot 'im," Ray said.

"Now there's an idea," I said.

"Hey, this girl?"

"Yeah?"

"Oh man. She's hot."

"I don't need the details, pal."

"Can you hang on? I gotta get a drink of water."

"No, I can't hang on. I'm coming up on Camino Capistrano."

"Oh, okay. Well, her name's Tamika. She's a guess-what."

"What would that be, Raymond?" My tone wasn't patient.

"A stripper. Down in Oceanside."

"Terrific."

"Yeah," he said cheerily. "What do you think?"

"I think you should be tied up and whipped hard."

"You want to come do it?"

"Goodbye, Raymond."

"Hee-hee," he said.

Off the freeway, I drove the quarter-mile down a road known only to shooters and people in search of nursery plants, kitchen tile, or getting their fenders fixed.

Sweeps of willow, mulefat, and oleander bushes waved in the wind on the left side of the road. The thick stands were perfect bedding-down places for illegals coming up from the southern border. Sometimes those voyagers crossing the tracks that zipper between the road and the distant cliff-side misjudge the speed of a train, and a tech like me is called out. Once, a man with an urge to self-destruct drove a shiny new car onto the rails and sat there, waiting. Ray says there's nothing like train deaths for mayhem, forget your mere murder. No one can imagine, he says. Problem is, I can.

When I pulled up to the square structure that housed the shooting range, I was still annoyed that Ray stood me up, but I had to smile at the thought of his last words to me on the phone. Ray with a stripper. Just like him. A stripper. Bless his little ol' heart.

Because, once upon a time, I myself had been a dancer on a low-rent stage—in Vegas, home to the bummed out, broke out, beered up, or bratty. Maybe I qualified as that last. I was a dancer, exotic, as they say. Get right down to it, a stripper, true and blue. Ray knows about the history, has the decency to refer to it only once in awhile and then only when we are alone. I was seventeen when I started. It was me. It wasn't me.

Today it seems simply not important. Murder is. Justice is. Serving and protecting, like Ray Vega and thousands of others do every day, is. If Ray-my-virile-buddy-Vega wants to date a stripper, well, we'll just let him.

I shot the Glock first and did pretty well on a target of a man in black silhouette, giving him a belt line and a happy-face, then took out my new "spurless" revolver with the hammer shrouded in the frame so it can't snag on clothes when used for a pocket gun. It was a long, hard trigger pull. When the gun finally fired, the muzzle-lift was so fierce the cylinder-release tore skin off my thumb-knuckle. I'd be shooting out street lamps before I'd knock over a bad guy. A young guy behind the counter in the check-in room was watching me through the glass. He put on a set of ears and came through the double doors into the gallery. "What you got there?" he shouted.

"S-and-W. It's cute, but I can't shoot for shit with it," I said, and offered the gun to him.

He aimed one-handed and fired five dead-center in the ten. "You're not used to the size," he yelled. "It's got a hell of a long trigger pull." Then he emptied the cylinder while holding the weapon *upside down* and pulling the trigger with his pinkie. The tight circle he cut was at the edge of the bullseye, three-o'clock, but a hell of a hole. He gave the gun back and said, "Anytime," then went down the row to see who else needed help or humbling.

Annoyed at myself, I clipped on a clean target, switched to the Glock, ran a new target out to fifteen yards, and cookie-cut the center so the backstop shone through like a camera lens.

From there I drove to sheriff's headquarters, just a couple of blocks from the lab, and sat through a class on audiology, otherwise known as forensic audiology, in a conference room cold as the morgue. I heard about waveform analysis and replication of acoustic events and waited for it to be over so I could warm up. Trudy Kunitz, another lab tech, sat beside me. She did a lot of police sketches of suspects for public release.

When the class finally broke we talked a while out in the

sun. Trudy had confided in me two weeks ago that she had tested positive for HIV. She was the sort to buy into the think-it-away school. I couldn't let her off without asking if she had the second test, intended to serve as a check.

She rubbed her arms for warmth, the sleeves of a heavy black sweater traveling up and down. Her glasses winged out thickly at the sides to correct for severe astigmatism. She said, "In my whole life I've had seven dates. Seven," she said, holding up fingers. "I'm thirty-four. Seven dates, two . . . events . . . and I get this." She shook her head. "I was a virgin till I was thirty, Smokey. No justice, not in this world. And it wasn't Katchaturian, if that's what you're thinking."

"I thought you liked him there for a while," I said.

"I had two lunch dates with him. He stiffed me for both. 'Fool me once, shame on you. Fool me twice, shame on me', right? Shame on me. Shame on me," she said, and turned to walk back.

I said, "I hear he's working for some magazine, writing articles on guns. I didn't even think he could spell."

She said, "Maybe you only need to spell 'Bang!' "

"You want to do lunch?" I asked.

"Can't make it," she said, her silver-daisy earrings swinging. "I have a post-post. A drive-by, courtesy of the Sixth Street gang. Then I have to take another blood test. Do you know how mortifying it is to even go in? These fascist women, sitting there talking to you like you're a little kid. The one who told me? She was younger than me! Heartless little Nazi. Tells me while she's shuffling papers. I had to ask her to repeat it, couldn't believe what she was saying, like she was saying go pick up a prescription or something. I didn't even like the sex. One time. That's all it takes. Shit. Let's go."

I walked over to Civic Center Square, on my way to a hot-dog wagon. Office people, lawyers, clerks, and clients, were emptying from the buildings for lunch. I bought a chili dog and a lemonade and sat on a cold bench with a pigeon perched on the other end.

He hopped down and waddled away but was back soon, with a mate. She was a beauty: black spots on soft white. Rock doves, they're called. They stood in front of me and sort of purred. Sucker that I am, I plucked bread and tossed it. In a flash, more birds landed. I licked the chili off one end of the bun and tossed more bits to them. Mistake. Half a dozen sailed in this time, dodging between people to head my way.

When I got back to the lab, I completed log sheets, made sure my lifts and print cards were in order, and was about to go to the computer when Stu came by. "You need to go out to Turtle Rock," he said. "We've got a dead male Hispanic. Timmins is tied up, King's at a doctor's appointment, and Kunitz I can't get hold of."

"Another one? Is it a Doe?"

"If it's a Doe, you phone me. I don't know if it's a serial or what, but I am not a happy camper here. I want thoroughness here, right?" I was about to come up with an appropriate answer when he asked, "Where were you this morning?"

"Audiology seminar, headquarters."

He frowned, recalling, then said, "You know where that's at, Turtle Rock?"

"No problem, Stu."

"You could see if Sanders is free to go along."

I nodded, not sure if Stu didn't trust me for the job alone or what, but not wanting to give it much thought, either.

Joe was on the phone when I came by. When he got off I

said, "I'm on my way out to a case," I said. "Stu says you'd be good company."

"Where's it at?"

"Turtle Rock."

"That's near David's school," he said, straightening his desk to leave. "We talked this morning. He said one of his roommates has been ripping software programs off the internet. Trademarked programs. That makes it illegal. I told him to give the jerk an ultimatum: Knock it off or move out."

I was pleased David confided in his dad. Joe's forehead was still pinched. "What's the matter?"

"Nothing."

"Why are you frowning then?"

"I'm not frowning. It's how you look when you get my age. You'll learn."

"If that's a bid for pity, it's wasted."

He got up and removed his jacket from the back of the chair. "I could have told him to report his roommate to campus police. I should have. I'm slipping. But you get to thinking, we got cases like this," he said, nodding to the phone, "and cases like your Doe's, and who gives a shit about some software programs?"

"Life in the big city," I said, rising.

"Eight million ways to die," he said. "Who said that, anyway?"

"The eight million? Mystery writer," I answered.

"Eight million. We've got what?"

"Two-and-a-half."

"Two-and-a-half million ways to die in this county. Most of them are not going to be by someone else's hand, and by someone we're supposed to trust, like this Dana Point asshole." He tapped a file on his desk. "Who'd you say wrote that, the eight million?"

I dug for my sunglasses. "Lawrence Block. He's got this guy named Scudder, a reformed drunk walks around New York doing favors for friends."

"Good writer?"

"I like him."

"How much you think a guy like him makes a year?"

"I wouldn't know."

"I should quit," Joe said, "write books."

"Mysteries?"

"Nah. I don't much like fiction."

"What, then?"

"Beats me."

"That could be a problem."

He pulled out the middle drawer of his desk. "Who's on this from Homicide, you know?"

"Will Bright."

"That girl's case . . ." he said, and struggled for the name.

"Nita Estevez," I said.

"That's the one." He stared at me the moments it took him to remember that night I spent complaining in his arms about how I couldn't get anywhere on that case, and how Will Bright wasn't giving it any more time until new leads turned up.

"Little Crane," I muttered as we headed out the door.

"Beg pardon?" Joe asked.

"Nevermind."

CHAPTER 6

"If that's a turtle, I'm a pterodactyl," Joe said. He held our two evidence kits in each hand, raised his elbows and cried, "Squawk!"

I snapped his picture.

We were at the corner of Rockview and Rocky Knoll, looking at the massive stone named for a turtle. It sat on a hill in a tailored community called Turtle Rock, which sat on a hill itself five miles in circumference. Surrounding it were farmers' fields and the expansive college campus of the University of Irvine, where Joe's son David was a sophomore. Bright flowers, vivid grasses, and yellow scene tape reading POLICE LINE DO NOT CROSS and *POLIZIA NO CRUZAR* gave the whole lump the look of a decorated cake.

The victim lay in shadow under the neck of the rock, on his side, eyes partly open. Blood had coursed across the nose and under the eye nearest the ground. A red kerchief spanned his forehead, blackened in the center from a round between the eyes. He had on a black jacket, a gray T-shirt with a design of a cannabis plant in the center, jeans with pale wear-marks at the knees, and white socks showing above black sneakers.

Linda Givens, a coroner's investigator, glanced up from her notes and said, "Hi, guys." In her forties, she was rumored to be an information hoarder, a non-team player.

Beyond her, on a curving path through the tended lawns of condos, a cop stood talking to a couple, the woman gesturing broadly as all three faced our way.

Joe sat on his heels near the body.

"Over there," Linda said, nodding toward some cards on a flat paper sack. The reporting officer had laid out the ID found on the body, she said. I said I wished people would leave the scene the way they find it. "Yeah, well," she said, shrugging. Investigator Bright had been there and left, she said, court date.

We stood before a small white sign stuck in the ground a few yards from the rock that said not to walk on the rocks because they were sacred to Indians. I asked Linda if she'd seen any spent shell casings, but got no answer. Maybe she didn't hear me. She folded her notebook and walked around to the accessible part of the rock and started up it, defying the Indian admonition. No more from Linda.

I gloved up, then moved to the collection of ID cards. Held just right, the first few cards showed friction ridges, but they could be the officer's fingerprints if he had been careless.

"Problem?" Joe said, coming toward me. Light see-sawed across his tie-clip shaped like a revolver.

"Look at this," I said. "A stack of ID's. Different names on the driver's license, Alien card, and a Sam's Club." The photos showed a man with high cheekbones, flared nostrils, and meaty chin: the victim beneath the rock, but which of the names was his? "Doe Three," I said, "until we know better." Pointing to the signature at the bottom of a card, I said, "Hector Estancio Rivera Rios. My Nellie Gail victim was Hector Rios. The victim Sunday, off Alton, he was a Hector too. Hector Gonzales, Hector Flores."

"Hannibal Hector?" Joe said.

I gave him a look. "Fun-nee," I said. "This one, the driver's license: the name's Alfonso G. Abrigal. It could pass in a dark bar with a blind bartender maybe, but the glue even shows through the lamination. Stu's gonna shit a brick."

"That's scary to contemplate," Joe said.

"He's probably got some high-priced profiler on the payroll already." I slipped the ID cards in the paper sack and marked it.

Joe said, "Stu's an old hand. He's not going to jump to conclusions at this point."

"Right. But Stu's afraid of the sheriff, who's afraid of the public. I just hate to catch flak when I don't deserve it."

"The public doesn't give a damn about dead illegals," Joe said. "It's the live ones they worry about, stealing those sought-after dishwashing and gardening jobs right from under our noses."

I said, "I read in the paper that by the year 2010 there will be forty million people of Hispanic origin in the United States."

"Less three," Joe said, then went to scout for evidence in the grass while I snapped off near shots of the victim. I did a close-up of a tattoo on the back of the victim's wrist: a spider with a red hourglass on the abdomen.

When Joe came back, he brought Linda with him and said, "Let's turn him." They tipped the victim face-forward so his own stiffened weight formed a sort of bent triangle braced on the ground. The rear pocket showed a diagonal outline, short-pencil size—syringe size.

"Careful," I said.

Joe glanced at me, held my gaze, and said quietly, "I know."

Bad things come in pockets. Those who cared to speculate on how Oakland Police Officer William John Brandon encountered the bug that canceled his life guessed it was a prick from a creep's pocketed needle.

My Bill, at twenty-eight. I am older this minute by seven years than he ever got to be. We had only six months together as husband and wife. The virus had only just been labeled, a form of raging hepatitis that took him away in just 48 hours. To this day I sometimes find myself watching behaviors in people who seem to have been around too long and wonder what went wrong with the universe that this lousy deal was struck.

Because I was a patrol officer then, I learned the name of the creep who owned the dirty needle: Daimon Sherman, and he'd been popped before, for sale of a controlled substance. For two weeks after Bill's death I went to Daimon's neighborhood and sat outside his house. He lived with his family even though he was 26 years old. He had a little girl, 12, already pregnant, only I didn't know that then.

Every noon, every evening after work, I'd come by. Noon, I'd be in my patrol car, the one Bill and I used as partners. I'd sit under the shade of a tree, watching the side mirrors, watching ahead, waiting. When Daimon Sherman came out, I'd trail him, slow, in my unit. I'd coast alongside not saying a word. He'd say, "*What?* Why you doggin' me, Officer?" He'd go in a store, out of the store. I'd be there. What was I going to do? I didn't know. Scenes would play in my mind: there'd be some challenge from him. When the time came, however it came, I'd step over his sucking body where it lay.

I remembered times Bill had gone easy on people like Daimon, and times he didn't yet was fair and honor-bound anyway. And I'd remember him at home, not a cop but a man and a boy and a lover and friend. When I saw Daimon Sherman, hatred hummed in my veins. I felt apart from myself, yet didn't care.

One day at dusk Daimon ambled down the street, stopped, turned, and threw his arms forward at me in a firing stance, eyes glaring. Just as quickly, he straightened and walked away down the sidewalk. A few steps more and he did something close to a break-dance, only he couldn't quite bring it off and he stumbled and lightly cracked his chin.

The next day I went again, but something in the ceremony was gone. Maybe it was seeing Daimon stumble. Two other times, a week apart, I went back to sit in front of the house. Then one day I gave up going to Daimon's.

Three weeks later while with my new partner, I got winged by a woman with a derringer in the bedroom of her home. One doctor worried that a bone chip might have lodged near my spinal nerve and could work its way in and leave me paralyzed. The whole thing built: Bill's death, the winging, Daimon's surprise fake-draw in front of his own house, the general accumulation of sights, scenes, and stories—so that by the next month, I handed in my badge. My sergeant tried talking me out of it, but not very hard.

Judging the path of the bullet, Joe said we might find the slug somewhere off to the right of the turtle. After collecting blood samples from the ground beneath the rock and the rock itself, I walked the area. Among some ground cover was a foil coffee bag. I placed a marker, shot more frames, then called Joe over. With him came a deputy coroner named Jared. The packet was open, only folded over at the top. I uncreased it and took out one of several smaller packets. "Condoms," I said. "What do you make of that?"

"If they're not jumbo I can't use 'em," Jared said, then flushed bright red. He was soft-looking, with mousy hair and a mustache that didn't do anything for a face that would ever remain ordinary.

I laughed and got an evidence bag to put the sack in. Jared said we should come down to the bottom of the hill. There, he pointed to a black cigarette pack with a Harley-Davidson logo on it.

"I didn't know H-D made cigarettes," Joe said.

"I might get a pack for Biker-Taz," I said.

"Give him one of *those* too," he said, pointing to the bag of condoms.

That afternoon I faxed copies of all the ID cards from the victim over to Homicide, then processed the H-D cigarette box and the coffee bag that held thirteen virgin condoms in foil by putting them in an airtight container next to a gel pouch called Hard Evidence, a cyanoacrylate compound. The fumes turn prints into nice white, visible ridges photographed with ease.

At the end of the day I drove over to the morgue, got buzzed in, and walked down the hall toward the autopsy suite. Cliff Yaroshak, chief coroner, was standing behind his desk reading a note as he slipped one arm into his gray suit jacket, preparing to leave. Lean and intense, he was my idea more of an FBI agent than a coroner. I asked where I could find the schedule for the three Doe's. He checked a log on his desk. "Tomorrow, eight A.M., for Sunday's and yesterday's."

"And today's?"

"Check with me later."

"This is the third Doe in three days."

"I'm aware of that," he said. "We also have an officer-involved case and eight new ones. I've been back East, just got in this afternoon, barely had time to get briefed. What information is developed so far?" He moved toward the doorway, waiting for me to go through first. In the lobby, he waved goodbye to the remaining office clerk.

"ID is going slow," I said when we got outside. "We have multiple names on each Doe and we're backed up to get prints from AFIS because the system's been down."

He pinched his lower lip. "This is not good." The sun behind him backlit a single long gray cloud, but his brow eased when he looked at the sky which was now turning pink from the receding sun and said, "I'm going flying right now. That's *my* relaxation." He made a move to go, then turned his head as though he'd heard a whistle. "You'll check with me soon as you run those prints, won't you? No pressure, now."

"Pressure? What pressure? Just pile another stone on my chest," I said, and threw my arms out in a cruciform.

On the way home I listened to an audio tape of a Western novel I bought at a used-book store, but five minutes of "I reckon" and I popped it out and put music on. I tried to think about what I wanted for dinner, couldn't decide. Wondered if my neighbor, Mrs. Langston, needed her dog walked. Wondered if my guinea pig was huddled in the dim light with his hard eyes gleaming. Reckoned he was.

CHAPTER 7

The next morning I was moody for reasons I couldn't pinpoint when Joe slapped a manila envelope down on my desk and said, "Turtle Rock prints. Linda sent them over."

I picked up the envelope and said, "To you?"

"What's wrong with that?"

His jacket was off, revealing a shirt still stiff from the cleaners.

I said, "The first two autopsies are scheduled for this afternoon. I'm meeting with Homicide before lunch."

"Good," Joe said. "Ferris has been all over the place this morning," he said. "He's behind closed doors with Watkins. I think it's on the Doe cases." Ferris was our lab director, Watkins the assistant sheriff.

Tipping my head toward the manila envelope, I said, "These people, they're like ghosts on the landscape. We care about how many cases we clear, how good we look to the higher-ups, how good the higher-ups look to the public, but that's about it."

Joe stood and tapped my desk with two fingers as he turned to go. "Give me a buzz if you get bogged down."

I gathered up my folders for the three cases. Inside were cards bearing lifts from the ID cards and photos of the fumed prints from Turtle Rock that a guy in Photo working swing developed for me already. I took them to the copier to enlarge five times, then put the copies under a light-box to trace the prints using a felt-tip pen because the ridges are often broken or faint. That done, I would return to the copier to reduce the copies back down, making for a strong, clear image with all the ridges, loops, and whorls now of similar weight and ready to scan into AFIS, which connects to the state's database containing prints for anyone who was ever booked for criminal activity, ever applied to be a teacher, wanted to join the military, or stood in line for a driver's license.

While I worked, I thought again of Little Crane. Maybe it was disrespectful to think of Little Crane by anything but her given name. But the frailty there, the memory of her being abandoned in a pitiless world, stirred me and frightened me and maybe touched a memory of someone I had known or been.

On my last run to the copier Stu came around the corner. We danced a little, then took our stances opposite each other against the walls. He said I was to meet with Homicide on the Doe cases. I said I already knew. "A citizens' group from Cypress is raising heat," he said. His hands served as cushions behind him as he bounced rhythmically off the wall. His forehead and nose gleamed from oil. "I got nothing against minorities, you know, but sometimes they leap to conclusions."

"They might have a history to justify that," I said.

"Yeah, well, we all have histories."

I gave him a quick run-down on how much of the evidence I'd processed. Then he said, "Do your business over there and get this wrapped up, okay? If you need to put a bomb under Homicide, then do that. The tail can wag the dog if it needs to. You need my help, let me know. We have other homicides over the weekend to deal with, in addition to other felony stuff. You cool on this?"

"I was thinking Trudy might—"

"Fine. I want to be sure she keeps busy. She's been taking a lot of time off lately. Maybe she doesn't have enough to do."

"It's none of my business, Stu, I realize, but she wouldn't be on a list or anything?"

"List?"

"For layoff."

"She's got seniority over *you.*"

"Oh, is that the way it is?" I was smiling but also fishing. He returned a half smile. "Do a good job on these Doe's."

"Or else," I said. His look said it could be a possibility.

And thank *you* very much, Stu, I thought, how's retirement sound to *you?*

When I made it to the copier Trudy was there, lifting the lid and putting a book on the plate. She had just punched the Start button. With the cover plate not all the way down, the escaping light washed over her. "Trudy," I said, "how goes it? Hoo, you're looking spiffy, now." She was dressed in black and cream and had a silver pin of a woman holding a parasol in her lapel.

"Why, thank you, Madame," she said, removing the book and the sheets in the catch-bin. "It's all yours."

I read the title on the book, and commented. "*Pathways to Ecstasy.* I think there might be rules about porno on the job."

"It's on controlling your destiny," she said. "I can lick this," she whispered, "I can." Then she fled down the corridor to the office with the letters on the glass spelling HOMICIDES R US.

Boyd Russell was in the middle of a spiel when I walked into the conference room at sheriff's headquarters. He was decked out in his usual brown suit, beige shirt, and yellow tie.

Will Bright was dressed in blue, even down to a needle-thin blue stripe in his shirt. His trim black beard and curly hair framed a watchful face. When I walked in he'd kept his

60

gaze on me without qualm.

He lifted his briefcase from the floor and took out a folder. "I don't know how you want to handle this," he said to Boyd, "but this is what I've got." He slid a computer printout over to Boyd and kept one for himself. I got none. Investigators are the top of the working-cop's echelon; minions like me don't count. I said, "You have an extra copy?" Will flipped the folder open with one finger and handed me a sheet, no apology. His glance told me a little test had just been executed.

The chart listed the three Doe's and characteristics of the scenes. I liked the layout but saw nothing new, and said so.

"Twelve thousand of the little buggers every day," Boyd said while reviewing the page. "Crossings are down from last year, but this is what we'll be seeing till somebody gets smart and plants spiked trenches and a few fragmentation mines. Twelve thousand on public dole, sooner or later. Your tax dollars and mine."

Will's gray eyes slid in their sockets like bubbles in a level to gaze at me then settle on Boyd. "More Russian immigrants collect welfare than Mexicans."

I said, "Trying to get by in a tough world."

"Yeah, well, let 'em get by in *your* back yard," Boyd said, and slipped off his jacket. "You want to talk to some of those people live around San Diego sometime? Wetbacks creeping through their yards at night. Shitting on lawns, stealing whatever's not nailed down. A whole farm family was killed a couple years back east of San Diego."

I told him I didn't think that case was proven to be from migrants. But it did seem the program called "Operation Gatekeeper" the INS put in place, to be enforced by Border Patrol, only strung migrants out more along the 1800-mile border between Mexico and the United States, driving them to more perilous routes. They died in deserts and the unpredictable currents of the Rio Grande. Sometimes they fell into the hands of human coyotes more wanting of conscience than their animal counterparts. And sometimes they fell victim to American citizens tanked on twelve-packs and carrying .45's who picked them off like target practice.

"Go where you ain't supposed to, take the consequences," Boyd said. "I bet you vote Democrat, too."

Will said, "Can we get back to the business at hand, please? This first one in Irvine. . . ."

"He worked at a place called Tri-Cycle, recycles copier cartridges. But that doesn't mean Doe no mo'," Boyd said.

Will said, "This one in Laguna Hills? Witnesses?"

"Aa-a, them rich people never get outta their limousines," Boyd said. "That's up in Nellie Gail. You been there?"

Will was new to the county. He ignored the question and asked me, "What do we have for prints on these?"

"Nothing for a couple of days. They're not even rolled off these two first victims, just the Turtle Rock."

He shifted in his chair. So far he wasn't impressed. "Okay, a weapon was recovered on the second one, right?"

I answered, "There's no blood or tissue on it but it definitely has been fired. I can tell you this: If it was the victim's, he didn't fire it the day he died. There's no gunshot residue on his hands. No prints on the magazine, none on the remaining rounds. Plus, no casings. I took a slug out of the tree behind him—"

"Firearms put it as a thirty-eight," Boyd said.

"It's awfully hard to tell from a deformed blob of lead without a barrel to connect it to," I said. "There's not that much difference between a .357 non-mag, a 9 millimeter, or a .38 Special—as I'm sure you know."

Boyd shrugged and said, "Talk to Firearms, then. It's

what they told me. Turtle Rock's a bigger problem, looks like."

Will raised his eyes to me. "You didn't find a slug, a casing, a weapon on this Turtle Rock."

"That's right," I said.

"How hard did you look?"

"I beg your pardon?"

"How thorough a search did you do?" I wondered what kind of Adam Henry this guy was going to be, A-H for a certain hidden part of the anatomy. *He* had been the investigating officer there, gone by the time Joe and I arrived. He waggled his pen. "You use a metal detector? You need to use a standard ten-inch searchcoil capable of detecting a slug tunneled to several feet."

"Wal, out here in the sticks, we don't have nuttin' near like that so new-fangled and all," I said. We did, but I wasn't going to go into details, not with this guy.

Bright put his pen down and raked his eyebrow with a finger. I expected the worst. But he said, "I've had a tough two weeks. Shouldn't take it out on you. I apologize."

I gave that brief thought, then said, "Welcome to Orange County Crimebusters."

Boyd winked at me, and we went back to the chart. He said, "These could be gang pops, but I tend to think it's personal. Up close on all three, the doer was having a conversation. No graffiti around. None of these are Santa Ana, after all."

Will dragged the end of his pen down to Doe Three, yesterday's victim. "What's this with the condoms?"

I said, "Found in a coffee bag, under a bush."

Boyd said, "Maybe they're one-fifth a rubber glove."

I took a hard candy out of my jacket pocket and picked red lint from it. "Can we go back to Doe Two, Nellie Gail, the grocery store coupons we found in the wallet."

"Juan Two?" Boyd said. He sang the melody of an old tune, "Juan-Two-Three, look at Mr. D.," in a surprisingly pleasant voice.

"Okay, what about the coupons?" Boyd said, finding his notation on a small notepad.

"I was wondering if you wanted to take them back to the store along with the sketch of the victim, see if any of the checkers might remember him."

"A thought," Boyd said.

Will said, "I'm surprised you didn't do that already."

Boyd's forehead reddened.

It went on like that, Will like a nettle under the skin, Boyd impatient in his own way to get this meeting over with. We ended it with no better feel for the cases, but at least we made a pass at communication that our respective management could note as progress.

In the hallway, Boyd said to me, "I'll have that guy for lunch."

"You're taking him to lunch?"

"Hah!" he said. "Fucking Adam-Henry."

"That's what I called him."

"To his face?" Boyd asked, ready to offer respect.

"Not yet," I said. I was nearly out the front door when I heard him call my name.

He hustled over, his jacket back on. "Your boss called. Doe One and Two, guests of honor."

"Now? They're doing the autopsies now?"

"Hey, I'm just the messenger. Want a ride over?"

"I've got my car, thanks."

He looked at me a second longer. "Sure?"

I remembered Joe's warning about Boyd's wandering ways.

"See you there," I said, and moved along.

64

CHAPTER 8

The room smelled strongly of meat. On the table near the door lay a large man discolored to a grayish-purple around the shoulders, sporting an erection coincident with his size.

A male coroner's assistant stood holding a twisted paper towel high in the air. With a lighter, he ignited the lower end. The paper caught, sending a ring of char creeping above the yellow flame as it climbed the torch. He held it over the corpse and plunged a knife downward into the dead man. Released gases flared like a barbecue coming on.

On the next gurney was an old woman waiting her turn, a "medical misadventure," then another male. He looked to be of Hispanic descent. The two at the end I recognized.

As I walked to meet Boyd standing at the back, assistants wearing plastic goggles and blue paper gowns, white booties, and pink masks were sectioning organs or weighing them in hanging scales, the women with their hair folded into clear plastic satchels.

Boyd was into a full yawn as I approached, perhaps from boredom, or perhaps from the discomfort most of us feel when in this room. He nodded toward the nearest gurney where a tech had her hands deep in the ditch of human organs. "X-rays show the bullet's still inside," he said. "Big guy on the end was found in a motel bathtub, meth smoker. Next guy drowned off Aliso Beach. Why is it Mexicans can't swim? They got an ocean same as us."

One of the techs gave Boyd a look, her dark eyes unreadable above her mask.

"Maybe we better look at that ankle," Boyd told Dr. Margolis, the pathologist working our case.

Dr. Margolis answered abruptly, "I wouldn't worry about it."

Boyd turned to me and said quietly, "I sure as hell won't."

The tech with the dark eyes went to the end of the table and lifted the head of the Nellie Gail Doe to slide a wooden block underneath. The block had a V-shaped cutout at the top so the head could rest without moving on its wooden pillow. Taking a comb, she parted the newly washed hair in a horizontal line mid-skull for the knife's path. In a moment she would slice through the scalp and peel the face forward in a procedure called reflecting, folding the face onto itself in a bizarre, other-worldly mask. Then the electric saw would whine through the sinuses for access to the brain. It was a procedure I never got used to.

"See you in a minute," I said, and walked away.

I approached the first table, where the pathologist was dipping a white plastic lid into the body cavity, then poured the collected blood into a small vial. She set the vial aside and came forward, her rubber gloves bright with fluid.

"Yours?" Dr. Schaeffer asked.

"The two on the end. How've you been, Doctor?" People who work at the morgue are a staunch lot. Some I wouldn't walk across the street with, but others I'd invite to my own funeral. This one I liked: Dr. Schaeffer-White, recently gone to just Schaeffer. She had two little girls and an ex-husband who'd grown tired of her workload and her evening studies at law school. He told her he'd seen her through med school, he wasn't going to do the same thing for law. She was living in a condo in Tustin Ranch about ten miles away, sharing custody in an informal way, but mostly still responsible for the kids with the help of a nanny from Guatemala. Her ex was engaged to a woman who designed bikinis.

She rubbed her forehead with a humped wrist and answered, "Not bad. What's new with you?" She turned to a tech and said, "Excise the track marks on that left arm, will you?" She stepped closer to me, her back to the table. "That one's a student at the osteopathic college. Very good. Very cute." I looked over Lenore's shoulder to see him take a scalpel and remove a plane of tissue from the corpse's midforearm. "What do you think?"

"I'm happy you see it that way," I said.

A crimp came and went in her brow, as if I either had poor taste or my mild remark could make her reconsider.

The whine of the saw had ceased behind me but the smell of bone dust was still in the air, and I wasn't quite ready to go back. As Lenore's cute student lay the strip of flesh on a tray, I asked, "Going to the wedding Saturday?" There was to be a merger of two coroner's technicians.

"Can't," she said, shaking her head hopelessly. "I have to study. Say, if you're going back to the lab, would you mind delivering a blood sample?"

"Sure, no problem."

The tech behind her placed the appendix he'd just removed in the sink and wrote "APP-yes" on the whiteboard against the wall. "I take the bar in July," Lenore said. "Ask me something, anything. I can tell you how to sue Santa Claus's sister."

"We'll be losing you," I said.

"I'll still be available for disaster work and maybe fill-in for vacations. We'll be able to get together." But I knew no matter how sincerely Lenore meant it she also didn't mean it, because she was entering law precisely so she *could* leave this work behind.

I went back to my cases. Dr. Margolis was in front of Doe

Two, dictating to a tech leaned on the counter, writing. "Deep muscle hemorrhage to the throat interior. Minor damage to the trachea consistent with strangulation, not sufficient to cause death." He said to Boyd and me: "We'll have a look at the contusions on this one tomorrow. By then they'll appear more clearly." Then he gave instructions to the techs to insert cornea caps containing small prongs so the eyes will stay closed. The other tech readied the waxed twine for sewing shut the mouth. The doctor handed me a plastic container with the deformed slug in it. I gave it over to Boyd and he looked at it without comment and handed it back. He took off his smock, a concession to protective clothing I didn't make, and wadded it up as we went to exit, coming too near the steel door of the cooler where bodies were kept so that it slid open as if by a bidding hand. The odor of preservation chemicals rolled out. "I have to get samples to take back to the lab," I said.

"Later, then," Boyd said, by way of goodbye.

Glancing at Lenore, still busy with the meth death, I stepped inside the cooler. Full house. Bodies lay on gurneys wedged under long shelves horizontal to the wall, with more on the shelves. On a shorter shelf were the tiny forms of two unclaimed babies wrapped in cold plastic instead of soft layettes. Next to them, fetuses hunched nut-like in formaldehyde solution within glass gallon jugs.

I found the vials of blood for Dr. Schaeffer in two labeled paper sacks sealed with green tape, then went to a supply room to get similar packaging to hold my bullet in its case. When I came out Dr. Schaeffer was near the gurney weigh-station doffing her protective clothing. When she slipped off the hair hood, her ash-blonde hair, close in color to my own, swung around a square jaw. Diamonds in a setting that spelled "Lenore" winked in from a gold chain around her neck. Her soft pink dress made her look like any preschooler's mom, not someone who was only a moment ago up to her elbows in blood. At the end of the hall, holding the inner door for me, she said, "Three months, Smokey. Can I last?"

"Sure you can." I signed out at the desk. She didn't.

"If I don't ace the bar exam on the first try, I don't know what I'll do." She held the door to the parking lot for me too. "This July. I just have to show the sonofabitch."

"That would be your husband."

"You met him once, didn't you?"

"He seemed nice enough to me," I said, aware that people don't want you to verify their own bad opinion of an ex. It reflects badly on their choices.

We were by the line of cars parked in front of the building. I stopped at mine. The sky was a pale gray slate. A chilly mist blew in our faces. "Should've brought my sweater," Lenore said, rubbing her arms as she looked back toward the morgue. She was still on the sidewalk when I unlocked my car door.

I said, "Why don't you go take your buddy in there to the movies," I said. "Or the tennis courts. Something."

"Not yet," she said, and gave a quick smile and turned away.

As I pulled out, a white bus with a sheriff's star on the front stopped at the gate to the Intake Center. Inside were inmates arriving from outlying detention facilities or returning from a work crew, many with Hispanic features under shocks of dark hair. Some might be from this same area of modest frame houses. As children they may have walked these same sidewalks to school. How many would wind up like the two young Hispanics I just left, covered with white plastic and lined up like piano keys in a morgue refrigeration room, feet exposed and a toe wearing a red-bordered WARNING tag attached by thin wire to forbid unauthorized disposition. Even in death, captive.

For my Juan Does presently being showered down for the final time outside the back doors of the morgue, the strenuous swim was over. They would not go on to wash cars, bus tables, work fields, pound nails, cut lawns, and join in a massive labor force without which the texture of Southern California life would not be the same.

Some of the men on the bus were gazing my way; others stared straight ahead. In a moment I would be in motion, driving away, free, making the most minor of choices they could not, while next to me sat the sacks holding human blood and the small, quick, cruel agent of another human's destruction.

I felt a surge of futility, as I often do when coming away from an autopsy. No one escapes. Does any demise matter over any other? It's easy to reach a place where it seems nothing about a victim's life has any more meaning than its violent end, as though that person were merely born to be murdered.

I drove, thinking about Lenore Schaeffer struggling toward her Great Escape and wondered if there were such a path for me. I thought of my colleagues sinking under the weight of a workload that seems with passing weeks to only gain the momentum of a landslide. Then there was Joe and the toll this work had taken on his marriage and maybe his son. I wondered what this work might be doing to me unseen, like a destructive cell bent on proliferation.

CHAPTER 9

Farmer flushed an egret. It sailed through the dank air like a slow-moving white paper airplane. Then the setter came trotting back, grinning as only dogs can do, and with muddy feet clear up to mid-leg. Farmer belonged to my neighbor, Mary Langston. She was a dear old lady who suffered from a connective tissue disorder called fibromyalgia. Now and then I offered a dog-walk. Something about an animal makes you remember it's good to be alive.

When I brought him back it was dark. I hosed him off good by the side of the building where a light shone over the faucet. At the top of the stairs by Mrs. Langston's door was a wicker chest for his towels. I dried him off before I rang the bell. Mary asked me to stay. *Jeopardy!* was playing on the TV behind her. I promised another time.

At my condo I fixed something to eat, bringing my guinea pig's cage into the dining room so he could watch; I was *his* TV. His name was Motorboat, from the long, burring noise he made when I touched him. Honey-blond all over, his consistent coloring causes the type to be known as a "self." Farmer found him. He's a blond puff with a round nose and rump, no tail. I had to drive to a vet to ask what it was. Now his home is a brown wire cage in the laundry room. He eats continually and pees constantly, but I am its mama now and it may be the only child-thing I'll ever have.

While I took care of the dishes I kept thinking I should have stayed longer at work to prepare the Turtle Rock prints. A news program on the television highlighted an actor's group calling for more representation in film.

I was late to work the next morning. By my desk I smelled a spicy aftershave: Stu had been there. I went to the coffee room and hauled a full cup back to my desk and drank it while shuffling through the self-generating paper in my "IN" bin. Parthenogenesis, it's called: the ability to reproduce without a fertilized egg. Handle a piece of paper once, time managers say. But I put most of the stuff back in my bin, got out my Turtle Rock cards, dropped my empty foam cup in the wastebasket, and headed for Joe's office.

He was just pulling a ceramic cup out of his drawer and a bottle of water. A packet of antacid discs lay on his desk. He slipped the seltzer disks in his cup, watching it foam. "David is failing school. Wants to quit entirely." I pulled out the guest chair and sat. "We had dinner last night in Laguna. Nice sunset, a little jazz combo playing. Then this."

"Get thee to a counselor, Counselor. Think that would work?" He gave a not-very-convincing nod. "I've got all these Doe prints to run," I said. "Unless I can talk you into it."

"Nice try," he said, and followed me to the doorway.

Two hours later we were still sitting at the CAL-ID computer monitor. It was slow with its searches that day. The green letters on black were blurring under my gaze. I stood to reach another copy of a fingerprint card when the last one came up nil. "Let's try this one," I said, and loaded a print onto the scanner, the one from the cigarette pack at Turtle Rock. Up came the white box labeled SEARCH PRINT IMAGE and the black maze of a fingerprint rendered from my earlier tracing. Next to it, another white square reading CANDIDATE IMAGE filled in with an image that had lain deep within the state's electronic storehouse.

Joe said, "Check it *out*," and pointed to the SCORE column, which reflects how many ridges, loops, whorls, arches, tents, radials, pockets, ulnars, doubles, and "accidentals" on the "unknown" fingerprint match up with the print the state has on file. The top score possible is 9999. Our cigarette pack delivered 8525. Subject's name, Froylan Marcos Cordillo, age twenty-two. Jacked a year ago for unlawful possession of a vehicle.

We put the card in for the prints rolled at the morgue. It came up Froylan Marcos Cordillo, but I could have made it easily just by eyeballing. Last known address, 34567 Marconi, Irvine. "Marconi," I said. "That's familiar."

"And cheese," Joe said.

"For that, you run these others alone. I'm going to get my notes." Before I got ten steps, I came back. "Joe, Marconi's in Technology Park. There are no residential streets there, no houses at all. That street does not run out of the park."

"Three-four-five-six-seven. We been had." Joe's face grew thoughtful. "This is on the Doe at Turtle Rock," he said, for confirmation.

"Right."

"Your Doe on Sunday was at Technology Park."

"Right."

"It would seem we have a connection, if we strain hard enough," he said.

I sat back down. "Let's do these others."

The computer was speedier now, for no reason we knew. Prints on the foil condom packets and coffee bag proved to be Cordillo's also, two others unidentified. I told Joe he could call Linda Givens with the news if he liked. He said, "Ohboy, ohboy."

We went our separate ways for lunch. About three, Dr.

Schaeffer called to say she needed tox results for the Technology Park Doe to complete her report; she couldn't reach our chief tox guy. I said I'd see if I could send it over and mentioned our fingerprint findings. Along the way in the conversation, her voice fell, and she said, "I have to do a baby."

"Oh, that's too bad," I said, and wondered why she was telling me this and why she was reacting that way; she's an experienced pro. Then she said it was her nephew and the parents begged for her to do it if anyone had to. "Say, Smokey? I'm wondering if you have a few minutes to maybe go have a drink sometime?"

That surprised me. We were friendly acquaintances, not friends, but I guess you have to start somewhere. I had an edgy feeling all the same. It felt like Trudy Kunitz all over again. People in pain, but their trouble, not mine. I'd heard of the concept of OPM: Other People's Money. You invest funds, build interest that's paid to you from other people's money. I came to develop one of my own: OPT, for Other People's Troubles. Usually I tried to keep their tales in a non-interest-bearing account so they wouldn't pile onto my own and sink the whole thing at an unexpected moment. But I could afford to be generous.

I was picturing her the way she usually was: a confident woman wearing her tasteful but definite diamonds while tending to the dead. Now here was a fragility so aching it seemed to quiver on the line, and a thought came to me from a book I read once by Nicolas Freeling saying that any woman is four or five women. "Lenore?" I said. "Say the word."

We met in the bar of an upscale sportsbar with green fern, glowing wood, etched glass, and guys scoping for women.

She said, "I had a case today with a guy's eyes blown clear out of his head. We think it was one of those Hydra-Shok bullets. Sometimes it kind of gets to you, you know?"

I'd seen the effects of those rounds on a gallon jug of water. "Do me a favor," I said, "don't tell me it was a Hispanic Doe."

"No, a Cauc. They've already made an arrest. Are you guys thinking you have a serial killer?"

"Anything's up for grabs at this point."

"Well, just remember Jack the Ripper did his jobs on six people in three months and then he was never heard from again. Maybe that will happen on these."

I laughed and said, "Looks like we're all getting a little desperate for answers, uh?"

We stayed and ate and gabbed and then, when she was feeling the glow from two good scotches I took her to a dive not far from Newport that has a small band called *Dead Heroes*. In a parking lot full of shadows, she asked if I was sure this was the place to be. I grinned and said of course it was. She kept bumping into my shoulder as we walked up the wooden pathway, while looking over hers. We passed 250 pounds of square meat who only said, "Good evening, ladies."

Inside, Lenore lit up the room with her bright pink suit, while I lay low in my dark jacket over a pale gray top. She drank a Stohle from the bottle and said, "Richard said he'd never date a woman who drank straight out of the bottle."

"Well, it's sure a damn good thing Richard's not here looking to get a date then, isn't it?"

"Damn right," she said, and took a slug.

The band was playing a not-bad rendition of "Owner of a Lonely Heart." In a while she whispered, "Do you think it's safe to go to the john?"

"I think it's safe."

"Where's it at?" she said, looking around. I pointed to the

alcove and she slid off the stool and managed the course across the floor. When she came back she seemed refreshed and even a little more sober. We stayed while she told me about her growing-up years and I told her some about mine. We took girl-guesses about the assistant she liked at the morgue, and we stayed until the bandleader gave his Roy Orbison mimicry of "Pretty Woman," then Lenore began to feel queasy and I took her home.

I said goodbye after promising to stop by in the morning so we could get her car. Then I went home to my dark house and chirping guinea pig, who scolded me harshly for leaving him again. When I bent close, he ran from the smell of Other People's Smoke in my hair.

CHAPTER 10

Mist hung in the valley as I took Jamboree down to I-5, getting my speed up on a long stretch between fields where beans, cabbage, and every kind of pepper grow. Deep in the fields, white-shirted pickers—*rasperos*—were already bent low in the rows.

Had one of the Does labored there? What about Little Crane? Had she worked the fields before going to the garment factory? Had she looked at the profiles of massive, Spanish-style homes everywhere in this valley and wondered how so many, so very many people, could own them?

In the distance loomed the two largest free-standing wooden structures in the world, hangars built in the Second World War and covered in tin when steel was in short supply. They used to hold as many as six blimps in their bellies. Through their huge open doors clouds sneak in and drop rain inside.

Lenore was with me. We were headed to pick up her car. She asked me if I intended to stay in this work a long time.

"I have to hang around," I said, "just to piss off my boss."

She smiled and said, "Well, I guess you could always take up a sideline selling Rubbermaid products."

"Pardon?"

"You know what they're calling you, don't you? The Rubbermaid, darling. They're calling you The Rubbermaid, because of the condoms you found."

"I'll kill 'em!" I said, narrowly missing a car that cut into my lane. I flanked to the third lane and pinned the horn, while the guy stared stonily ahead.

Lenore rolled down her window and shot him the finger, then looked at me with wicked triumph in her eyes.

"Why, Doctor," I said.

"The jerk," she said.

I let her off at her car and went on to the lab, passing by a handful of pickets outside sheriff's headquarters. I couldn't read the signs because the traffic lights were in my favor.

Joe saw me bustling in as he was coming out of the coffee room and said, "Banker's hours."

"What are you, my spy?"

He tried to sip his hot coffee. "I've got meetings all morning."

"What do you think would happen if we called a moratorium on them?" I said. "Just say No More Meetings, and never go?"

"The world would implode," he said.

"I saw pickets down the street. Know what that's about?"

"No idea," he said.

I looked at him there, handsome in his blue shirt and said, "Hey, big fella, how'd ya like to come up and see me sometime?"

"I'm supposed to meet Jennifer. To talk about David."

"Ah." I started to ask about David again, but left it there. "Back to the trenches," I said, and went off to my desk.

I had an hour before I'd have to leave for the Turtle Rock autopsy. I stacked paper in *Now, Later,* and *Maybe Never* piles, then left the building and went to the morgue, thinking not only of my Does but of the terrible task that Lenore Schaeffer still had to face that day.

This time I turned right on Flower, taking a different route, and didn't see pickets outside any other county facilities. I did notice a marquee by bleachers in a small park squished between city buildings announcing a baseball game between county cops and Santa Ana's finest.

The autopsy took its course without notable findings, not even a captured projectile that did our Turtle Rock Juan Doe in.

After work I went shopping for shoes for the wedding the next day, bought some sexy lingerie too, at 60 percent off. If they can sell it and still make a profit at 60 percent off, why not offer it that way to begin with?

Joe called around seven. If I'd have him, he said, he'd be over. It was ix-nay with Jennifer that night. They'd argued over the phone. I put the shoes away, took a shower, looked twice at my fancy undies, cut the tags off. What's new duds if not to wear?

Propped on an elbow, Joe said, "Once upon a time. . . ."

(He was wearing no clothes.)

"Yes?"

(I was wearing no new lingerie.)

"There was a prince. A mature man, a manly man. Rippling muscles. Steely blue eyes—"

"This is a comedy, right?"

Joe kissed my nose. "You want a story, or you taking a deposition?"

"I'll behave."

In another time, another house, I had a mirror hung by a chain made of large gold links with a red wooden ball on the end. Depending on the company, I'd turn the mirror horizontal, hang it that way. Today there was no mirror, just a semi-settled-down me and a good man sixteen years my senior who was going to tell me a story from his vault of good ones or suffer an unmerciful end.

"This prince," he said, "he loved a beautiful maiden."

I kissed his hairy arm. "Enough about me. Go on."

"End of story."

"What kind of story is that? Come on."

"The maiden dumped him. Dumped him cold, for a knight with a fancy horse."

"The bitch."

He swept his hand over the downslope of my waist. A change came into his face, distant, thoughtful. His head wagged on the platform of his hand. Then he said, "Sorry. Preoccupied. Harold Raimey phoned today. He thinks it was the husband too. We just can't pin him. But it's got to be the husband."

"Sort of makes you double-think the concept of marriage, doesn't it? Why'd you stay so long in yours?"

"There was David."

"You're not supposed to stay for the kids. So say the experts."

He kicked off a knot of pine-green sheet. "An expert is a bastard with a briefcase from Boston."

"That's cute."

"It's not original."

He grew thoughtful again. "Why'd I stay so long . . . ? Fear and habit. Habit and fear. Not very flattering, is it?"

"Fear of what?"

"You name it. The big scene. How much her lawyer would stick me for. Not having anyone to go to the movies with. The in-laws—you get attached. Do you divorce them too? Of course you do. Your friends, the people you work with—you don't want to explain. It's embarrassing." He stroked my hand then said, "There's another reason I didn't want to leave. I was afraid some hot young thing would follow me home some night."

"It *is* a scary thought," I said. I studied the architecture of

80

his face, the brow with five lines of latitude, the smile that is his secret weapon, and said, "C'mere," and kissed him.

As if on cue, the phone rang. " 'Scuse me, Monkeytoes. Back in a minute." I leaned over the bedside and dragged the phone by its cord over the carpet from where I'd set it to make room for our drinks. It unplugged at the base. Holding up the end, I said, "With one swift move, the whole world disconnects."

"It should *be* that easy," Joe said. He was sitting up now.

When I plugged back in, the phone rang again. "Mama Corleone's Pizza," I said.

There was a pause, then a hesitant male voice. "This is Dave Sanders. Is my dad there?"

"Just a sec." Handing the phone over, I mouthed, "It's your son." David had never called my house before.

"Did I overstay my curfew?" Joe asked. He listened a while, then said, "Ten-thirty, eleven. Why? Is something wrong? I can be home earlier. You want to meet me at the apartment?"

"Go," I whispered, handing him his shirt.

He said into the phone, "I can be home in five minutes. Okay. Later, son." Handing me back the phone, Joe silently pulled on his shirt, shorts, jeans. Zipped, thought a moment, then said, "Now that was strange."

I fixed a cup of weak tea and went to say hello to Motorboat. He lay in cool moonlight, stretched long and comfy on his pine chips, eyes burning bright: the Thing That Never Sleeps.

"Chum," I said, "how you?" I lifted the cage lid and ran a finger and thumb along his soft log of a body. "*You* stay up all night thinking. What good's it do? Do you have any answers for me? Hm? No answers, not one."

CHAPTER 11

We went to the wedding that was also an excuse for a bunch of cop-types to get silly and rude. The hearse was parked outside when I arrived. It had purple lights on the back fenders and a pink-and-black "Just Married" sign anchored front and back. Joe was standing beside it waiting for me. I told him he looked snazzy.

"Snazzy? You look pretty snazzy yourself."

It was the first time I'd worn a dress in months: dusky pink.

We had talked earlier about what happened last night with his son, but Joe brought it up again. Joe said, "Maybe I've installed a hyper-conscience in my kid. Just by being around Greg he figures he's a criminal. This is the guy who's taking stuff off the Internet that I guess isn't licensed to him or something."

"I remember," I said. "And it certainly is illicit."

"Yeah, I know, but it's not murder," he said.

People in the house were leaning out the front window waving and calling to us to come in. "Looks like we better," Joe said, and bounced ahead.

"Where's Ray?" I asked.

"Flirting with the sweetheart he brought."

"Is it the stripper?"

"What stripper?"

"You don't want to know," I said.

Inside, the minister said we'd have a five-minute rehearsal in one of the bedrooms, and that brought a lot of catcalls from some of the wild partyers already blitzed from brews stashed in a coffin of Ray Vega's creation, lined with a shower curtain patterned with rotund naked women. On the top he had burned the words: *Ray's Dead-Drunk Liquor Store.*

The poor minister kept stroking his hair off his forehead and looking around as if he hoped he'd never have a need for the protection of anyone from Orange County law enforcement. When the ceremony and dining was over Ray made sure the man of God had a brew tucked in his pocket before he saw him out the door.

The bride's father convinced the couple to take his Lincoln instead of the hearse. Those of us who weren't shrieking in the hot-tub out back transferred signs and streamers while the couple stood in the kitchen with the parents, receiving sage advice.

Now Joe and Ray and I and a county sergeant named Gary Svoboda were ferrying the hearse to the ocean, three of us grinning like pigs on sour pears. Ray and I were in the back, Joe and Gary in the front. Ray sat on the floor of the hearse with his legs drawn up, his ivory jacket gleaming like a molar. I lay on the casket, bony knees hanging over the end. When our driver took a quick turn at the last light leading to the Dana Point marina, the melted ice in the liquor store beneath me sloshed.

"Whoa, little dogie," Ray cried, and looked about to retch.

"I oughta dump the whole lot o' ya in the ocean," Gary said, his beefy hands clamped on the steering wheel, gunfighter mustache twitching.

In a convertible next to us, two guys wearing ball caps were looking our way. One of them said, "What the hell is *that?*" Ray put his face to the window and gave them a dead man's stare.

Gary stopped the bus at the top of the bluff for a breathtaking view of the 2500-slip harbor, then drove a few blocks over to a three-tiered, tailored park with a winding path and a gazebo looking over the Pacific.

We piled out, walked to the gazebo, and gazed down on the mile-long breakwater and a replica of the Pilgrim, the stately, two-masted square rigger used by hide-harvester Richard Henry Dana.

The ocean was shearing its first slice from the bottom of the sun. The world looked more beautiful than any of us deserved.

Ray said, "Why didn't we get married here?"

"*You* didn't get married," I said.

"Oh thank God!" He looked at his white jacket, the front, the sleeves, and grinned. "Saved again!"

Then, for some reason inexplicable except to drunks, we all grew quiet. A para-sailor came floating in, slitting the skin of water. The red chute eased down above him, while farther out, a handful of white sails saw-toothed the horizon.

The hush of the sea, the gliding gulls, the mansions inland with their windows beginning to light from within, all this was too good to leave just yet. We went to sit on the grass among the tiny grass-daisies as the evening drew on and the colors palled and the diminishing scent of Gary's shaving lotion roped us together. Gary, solemn Gary, gave in and told a joke that didn't go over, but we laughed anyway. After a while, Joe took his jacket off and wrapped it on my shoulders. In another moment, he said to Ray and Gary, "A couple of blocks over, a man killed his wife while walking on one of these bluffs."

"Always on the job, that Joe," I said softly, and took his hand and bit his palm a little.

"Hey, you buttheads, we don't want to talk about work, do we?" Ray said.

I shoved a bare foot at him. He fended it off, leaned back, closed his eyes, and sang a pensive Willie Nelson about when the evenin' sun goes down, it's the night life, not the right life, but it's his life. Joe hummed too, and Gary, his eyes focused on the green-gray sea, nodded along to the tune.

I couldn't help it: I thought of my Does. No yachts with banners in a marina for them. Only the moon in its cool dispassion, and a slow-moving security cruiser behind us, checking to see that everything was as quiet, as barren and lifeless, as it was supposed to be.

CHAPTER 12

Thirty miles south, along San Juan Creek in San Juan Capistrano, an army of Audubon volunteers set out to hack plants invading the natural habitat of native birds, and I meant to join them.

I don't agree with all of Audubon's politics, attend no meetings, and know the officers' names only by newsletter. I am more bookish than fervent. Still, and in spite of a slight headache from debauchery, I decided I'd rather engage in bush wars than stay and do household tasks that put me in glum moods.

I gathered old gloves, a hat, and an insulated bottle painted in military camouflage I'd picked up at a garage sale. Before leaving, I looked in at Motorboat. He stared at me from the open end of a hollow log, his lower jaw shifting, the teeth ever in need of grinding. I said goodbye and told him to keep out of trouble.

I'd drawn a map to the cleanup site on a big yellow sticky and stuck it to the center of the steering wheel. I'd be making my turn onto Ortega Highway, one part of which is dubbed Ricochet Alley by members of the highway patrol because of the cars that careen off the roadside into the ravines below. At another spot known as Pushover Point junked and stolen cars, perforated by weekend shooters until they look like tea strainers, nestle in the shrubs.

Today I wouldn't be going that far. But just being on the road made me recall a murder scene Joe and I had covered where a man had been beaten, then strangled with a rig of barbed wire.

Before long, I was driving down a quiet road lined with oak, sycamore, and the aggressive foe I'd soon be fighting, the bamboo-like cane known by its scientific name as *arundo donax*.

In an open grassy area, a white banner was stuck in the ground identifying SOUTH COAST AUDUBON. At a table where a man and woman were deep in conversation about home plumbing fixtures I signed in, giving my name, address, and whom to contact if I should fall over dead by spider bite, wasp sting, or rattlesnake strike. The man pointed to some tools laid out on the grass: pruners, shovels, rusty rakes, and a machete. "Take what you want. The ones with orange tape belong to the district. Those without belong to J.G."

"Thanks," I said, and lifted a machete whose blade was nicked and streaked with plant life. I swooped it through the air, then decided I'd probably wind up chopping my own ankle instead of clearing bird habitat, so I put it back and opted for long-handled pruners. All around, volunteers were rustling brush and throwing cut trophies behind them. A couple of kids ran about. An old Hispanic man swung a machete with ease.

I walked down a shaded gully to a fortress of cane near an electrical tower and leaned my hat against a stump hollowed by decay. Inside, a bug turned frantically on a tiny lake of captured water. The cane stalks were gray at the base from mud-splash. I knelt and worked the blades of my pruners into a pack so tight I had to make two cuts before I could yank the first stalks out.

For two hours I cut, pulled, and manhandled cane. At times I'd think of my recent cases but tried to shunt it aside, knowing the mind needs rest so the pieces of puzzle can come vibrating home like shavings compelled to cleave to a magnet.

After a particularly strenuous fight with a stubborn stalk, I dropped my pruners and searched for my thermos, now buried in a fan of green leaves. I pulled it free, then glanced at the tiny bug still churning in the stump water, slipped off my dirt-heavy glove and dipped my finger into the lake to lift out the bit of struggling life. Wiping the creature onto the edge of the stump, I said, "Second chance, bub."

"Bulldozer coming through!" A sun-burnished man surveyed my pile of destruction. "You do that all by yourself?" He smiled, showing bright, even teeth. "My name's Gil."

"Smokey," I said, and uncapped my camo jug.

"Smokey?"

"I prevent forest fires." I took a drink, watching him.

He said he was recruiting to load the Dumpster.

"Sure," I said. We took the path, Gil leading. On a dry knoll the dark profile of a bird asserted itself, its tail high as it strutted in pace with us. "Brown-headed cowbird," I said. The female lays her eggs, one here, one there, in the nests of other species. Her young emerge first, then bully or starve out the other hatchlings.

"All I've seen out here this morning are blackbirds, scrub-jays, and a Tammy Wynette," Gil said. Creases formed at his eyes. "A Nashville warbler."

"That's bad, really bad," I said.

"I got a million of 'em."

"I'm sorry to hear that."

We headed for the brown sheet-metal container where a pickup piled high with cane was backed into the loading end. There was a man throwing stalks forward from the tailgate and another standing in the Dumpster to direct the flow.

The woman I saw at the check-in table came up, wiping her brow with her arm. "I'm taking the kids home for a bit, Gil," she said. "You want to tell people there's castor bean that needs to come out up on that rise?" I looked at the lady

88

with the red face and football-player legs, and thought I never would have made her and Gil for a couple.

Gil said, "I'll put Drew and Shannon on it, but we're just about full up here. We shouldn't pull any more."

"It really needs to come out, Gil," she said, then moved off.

I knew castor bean contains ricin, one of the world's deadliest poisons. Originally from Africa, a mere two beans could kill you. In Europe there was a famous espionage case in which a man was murdered by a tiny metal burr coated with ricin and jabbed into his leg by the tip of an umbrella as he made his way in a crowd. The mature plants look like old scrub, but the tiny shoots pull up easily from the ground. The woman called back to Gil: "And if you find any more dead bodies, do it while I'm gone."

I thought she was kidding, some joke about the castor bean. But then Gil said, "They found a body out here Friday." I felt numb but didn't show it. "Yeah. A guy and his dog found it."

"Where?"

"Down there by the creek. Lynelle's the one who told me."

Her small red pickup was just pulling away.

It wasn't unusual I wouldn't know about the case. With 120 people at the lab, any of us could be on a case and the news not get around until the next department meeting. But the location made me uneasy. "A transient, do you know?"

"I think so."

Then why *hadn't* I heard about it? Maybe it wasn't a Doe.

Gil climbed into the pickup bed when the one man jumped down to unload the wheelbarrow. I followed, then leaped over to the Dumpster where the second man was, and the three of us threw and caught stalk till the level at the back of the pickup was low and the back of the Dumpster was high. The man beside me began to trounce on the cuttings. I did it too. The load crackled like popcorn; you couldn't help but laugh, this odd trampoline.

Then Gil jumped over and the other guy got off, so it was Gil and me jumping and bouncing until the both of us were giggling and out of breath, flat on our backs and eyes away from the sun. When his gaze met mine, he said, "Nice to meet you, Smokey."

I got up and brushed my pants and said I guessed we'd better get back to the cutting.

He said, "We can't do any more, really. The city says we have to have it all picked up by the time we leave. Mike's going to stack it near the road and come back with the truck later." He jumped down and lent a hand. "How's lunch sound? There's fast-food places down the way."

"No thanks," I said. "I'll be seeing you, Gil."

"Maybe some other time?"

"I'm sure I'll run into you and Lynelle again."

"If you're thinking we . . . the two of us . . . ? Oh, no. Lynelle and I aren't together. Not me. Uh-uh."

I smiled but said thanks anyway. Gil was handsome, in a blond sort of way, but I was not in the market for a new man. I reached to get the pruners, and Gil came up again.

"I've seen you before," he said. "In Newport, at Back Bay. What'd I do? All I said was I saw you a couple of times."

"If you saw me," I said, "why didn't you say so before?"

"Whew, that pushed a button."

I looked around for my sunglasses, didn't see them. In my time, I've been stalked, followed, and discovered, all three. It doesn't take a lot to set my senses on alert.

"It didn't come to me, I guess," Gil said, "until we were back there at the Dumpster."

"What's your last name, Gil?"

"Vanderman."

I kept him in my vision while I still looked among the leaves.

"Lose something?"

"Sunglasses." As I lifted cane fronds, Gil lifted some too. I didn't need his help, didn't want him there. I finally found them wedged in leaves.

When I looked back at Gil, he was peering into the stump. Two gnats this time stirred the dark sheen of water. He dunked a twig and lifted out both bugs, blew on them, then flung the thing away, riders and all. "Ready?" he said, as if we were a couple going somewhere. Once in the clearing, he dug in a back pocket and opened a wallet, took out a card and handed it to me.

"What's this?"

"My card," he said, as if any moderately bright person could assume.

In the top left corner was the stylized head of a great blue heron. In the middle, *Gil Vanderman,* and under it, *Naturalist.* A phone, a fax, and the words *Tours, Photography, Lectures* completed the card.

"See, Smokey? There may be a dead guy in the culvert," he said, "but I didn't do it." His voice was softer, his eyes even kinder than before. He could be a Ted Bundy, that smooth style.

CHAPTER 13

Numero quatro.

In a storm drain off Ortega Highway, Juan Doe Number 4 was found lying face down in a couple of inches of water.

Trudy Kunitz was on it. "He had a good haircut," she said, "like from a salon, shaved close on the sides, with three horizontal lines above the ear." She said he still had a knit cap on, nailed by a bullet. T-shirt and jeans. Old dress shoes, no socks. There was a watch with a busted leather band and an alligator on its face. "I'm faxing the sketch to Homicide in about twenty minutes. They'll put it out to the papers tomorrow. You watch. That haircut, we'll get an ID overnight."

I said, "I took a chance somebody would be in who knew about the case." I was using my cell phone.

"Somebody was."

"Go home now, Trudy."

"It's like a tomb in here," she said. "Couple of guys in Tox, is all."

"Then I'd say it was time to go home."

She was silent a moment, then said, "It's worse at home."

As I drove north, I reviewed the cases like a journalist figuring the Four W's and an H: What, Where, Why, When, How. I added another: Who? Four GSW's to the face. All Does. *Why?*

I was nearing Technology Park. Beyond it, a blue cloud was poised over the twin blue humps of the Saddleback mountains like a stalled flying carpet.

Farther on, a single green tractor with yellow wheel-rims was perched, manless, in a tilled field.

Once I'd seen a man with a roll of plastic set upon his shoulders, the free end fleeing down his back and onto the cultivated rows to cover new plants as he slow-walked in silhouette against a gold sunset. When he was done the sheeting would turn these fields to lakes of silver.

Though I had just come from cane cutting, I longed to be out there, quiet, anonymous, fruitful. In the fields there's a willfulness of life that pleases me. A mouse daring a hawk. A stumbling beetle racing for shade. Poke a seed, spit on it, it grows. I wanted to be there, away from what mankind inclines to do to itself in all the varieties of cruel intrusion.

"How was cane cutting?" Joe said.

"Dirty, hot, and fun. You can join me sometime."

"Not on your life. A couch, a beer, a game, and thou, my dear."

I balanced the phone on my shoulder while I went to look in at Motorboat. Squinched at the back of his log, he pipped. I raised the cage lid. He darted out, then back. Guinea pigs should be called greased pigs. They go as fast in reverse as forward.

"I just talked to Trudy Kunitz," I said. "A body was found Thursday afternoon in San Juan Creek, down where I was working today."

"You have anything to do with it?"

"A card, that's what you are," I said. "Think of it, though. Another one. What the heck's going on?"

"Worry about that tomorrow. Today's still Sunday."

I let that sink in, then asked, "Okay, so what are you doing this afternoon?" He said he was going out with his son to buy tires. "Oh yeah," I said, "he told me about that."

"He told you?"

"At the parade."

"What a dummy, huh?"

"That boy's almost as smart as his father," I said.

He laughed and said, "I'm meeting him at Jennifer's. It'll be in the air, like our son wouldn't be acting weird if our marriage hadn't taken a left turn over Iceland."

"I'm sorry, Joe."

"I look at her, this woman I spent twenty-two years with, it's like I don't know her at all and wouldn't want to if I just met her. I wish her well, I want her to have a good life, but . . ."

"This is the first time I've heard you say anything the slightest bit critical, which tells me you're either a hero or you spent so many years together even her faults don't interest you anymore."

"It's called forgiveness."

"You're smart, sexy, and sweet, you know that, Joe?"

"Then why ain't I rich?"

"Ambition's about how sharp your elbows are."

"Are you saying I'm not ambitious?"

"I'm saying you're perfect the way you are."

"That all?"

When I came out of the shower I wrapped up in a robe, got a glass of milk, then went to check on Motorboat again. He was still hiding. I set the glass down and overturned his log and lifted him out. First he purred. Then he sneezed. It sounded like a hiccup. I brought him close to my cheek and felt his ears fiery on my skin. I got dressed, put him in a box, and drove to the emergency vet's.

"It's a *rodent.* Don't people hire exterminators for these

things?" I said when I was in the examining room.

The vet ruffled the tiny golden head, then stood him on his forelegs to inspect whatever's at the rear axle. Motorboat shrieked loud enough to make paint peel. "They chill easily," he said. "He's got a cold. Just keep him out of drafts and give him Vitamin C."

Back home, I brought his cage into the living room. I settled onto the sofa and watched a show on building an Adirondack patio chair, then turned pages in a book I'd gotten out of the basement library at the lab last week on taxidermy.

Late afternoon I felt at loose ends, so I put on sweats and a fanny-pack with my new S&W in it, and walked across the road to the bay. It's not so wise a thing to take a walk down its shrubby paths in the dimming light, but the 700-acre bay has a drawing power hard to resist. Days, it is host to bicyclists, boaters, fishers, joggers, and busloads of children on field trips. Nights, it seethes with a *mardi gras* of birds and beasts.

Before I moved here there'd been two murders, one a schoolgirl, another a woman with roses stuffed between her legs. The only trouble of late has been a few shouting matches between "wheelers" and "walkers."

The writer Marcel Proust had a horror of sunsets—so operatic, he said. I thought of that while I admired the brass-rose sky. In the air was a sweet smell of damp sage, tidal brine, faint decay, and cliff flowers.

An older couple came down the trail ahead of me. A dove that had huddled unseen on the graying path spurted off between us. The couple said there was a heron back there choking down crab like no tomorrow.

"Really?" I said. "I'll look for it."

They moved beyond me. Then the man looked back and

said, "It's getting kind of dark. I'd be careful if I were you."

The woman was a comfortable contrast, yet it was she who added, her forefinger raised, "You young people sometimes forget how bad it can be, all the weirdos in the world these days."

"Right," I said. "Have a good evening. I won't go far."

"That's good," they chimed.

CHAPTER 14

I wanted to see the ankles of Doe Two. The damage there might show more clearly now, this subtle development called a "second event." A coroner's deputy named Mona told me, "No problem," picked up a camera, and rose from her chair with an effort that strained her black twill pants. On her blouse was a large, brightly painted version of a carrot-haired Bette Midler. I commented on it. Mona got a satisfied grin on her face and said, "My alter ego."

In the cooler by Doe Two she folded the plastic cover down. "The marks do appear to be consistent with punctures from canine teeth," she said.

"But if that occurred after he was dead there would be no blood, right? There was blood."

"I'm not a doc but that would be my assumption. Here's something else," she said, "up here." She pointed to irregularities on the bridge of the victim's nose and under both eyes. "My guess is he was held tightly, very tightly, by some sort of binding. He could have been cuffed too. We have faint red at the wrists."

"Nothing like a belt or cuffs at the scene," I said. She just shrugged a shoulder and said she'd snap off some shots for me and bring them into the autopsy room, which was my next stop.

I said thanks and went on. The techs and docs were at their stations. Lenore was not among them. Trudy wasn't there either, whom I half-expected although it is not a requirement for the forensic jock to attend.

The San Juan Creek Doe was as Trudy described. Haircut. Young. Hispanic. Dr. Margolis was the examiner. Good. I asked if he saw similarities in any of these cases. He pointed to the hole in the forehead and said, "Other than that, no."

When Mona brought in the Polaroids, I asked him what he thought caused the marks on the face and ankles of Doe Two. "I'd guess it's a contusion from a leather belt," he said. "See this?" He spread his gown to show a brown belt with lacing top and bottom. "Something to think about," he said, then turned back to his work.

At a Fifties-style diner a few blocks away I ordered a bagel and cream cheese and coffee. Dishes clattered, voices screeched. I looked out at the blue, blue sky and had a sudden feeling of disassociation, as if I belonged nowhere. I watched people come and go, their conversations heard yet not heard.

A belt, I thought. Okay. Victim restrained, brought to that hill in Nellie Gail by the water tanks. No. Victim on that hill, then restrained, because he was carefully set against the tree, and it would be too hard to lug a bound body, living or dead, up the hill. Why there? What about the coyote bites?

I ate my meal but still sat there, tapping my finger on the side of my cup, unwilling to go. Then I had it: The boy was shot while restrained against the tree, and left for dead. An animal came by. It chewed on the boy's ankle, maybe trying to pull him down for better vantage. Perhaps the boy moaned. Perhaps the killer, still nearby, heard the moan, and came and sent a second round through the same portal as the first. But why, then, did I not find a second slug? No. The boy was shot. He did not die. Coyote came, sniffed. Bit. Boy, though unconscious, kicked. Coyote fled. Boy died. Coyote waits. Simple.

★ ★ ★ ★ ★

I left a message for Stu that I was going back out to Nellie Gail. I was glad he wasn't in because he would say there's no point. A crime scene opened to the public can no longer deliver anything to serve as evidence for prosecution. But I went anyway, to satisfy myself. This time I brought a magnifying glass to more closely inspect the bark on the opposite side where the body leaned. I thought I saw faint impressions but could not be sure. It meant nothing. Nor was any shooter hiding in the bushes. No one to throw his hands up and say you got me girl, I surrender.

Joe wasn't in his office when I got back, but later I saw him involved in conversation with a detective at the bench by the microscopes so I didn't go in. He left a message on my office voice-mail about getting together, and I left one for him. When I didn't hear again, I figured maybe something came up with David.

Late in the afternoon a colleague came by and told me she'd just come from a scene involving a starved and beaten child of four. The child was alive, the mother wasn't; she finally did the world a favor and drank strychnine. My colleague broke down at my desk. I held and comforted her. Then she said, "Fuck. I'm getting out of here," and left.

On my way home I kept switching the radio on and off. The sky was dark with threatened rain. I stopped to mail a letter and rent a video, and when I filled my tank with gas I kept an eye out, watched the shadows, saw in every car or crowd a killer.

Fifty. Five-O. Is it old? Is it young?

All I know is, no matter how I march the numbers forward or back, stand them on their head, measure them off like tick-marks on a ruler, fifty, blessed fifty, is too young to relinquish impact upon this world. Fifty is too young to die.

I was in the snack room the next morning around ten getting a cup of machine-dispensed chicken soup, reading a report at the same time from the FBI on how drug use is now higher in female juveniles than in males, and speculating on why that should be so. The cup of soup was scalding. I set it on the counter for a better grip so I could pour some of it off and add cold water, when I heard from the lips of a man in the hallway the words, "Oh, no! *Shit,* you say," in that distinctive tone that tells you he's just heard something you don't want to. Then all I caught was a word here or there.

But as the men moved past the aperture of the door, it was the last few words I heard that devastated my heart: "He was supposed to turn fifty next Monday, wasn't he?"

That would be Joe.

I shot out into the hall and caught up with them. These were men I didn't know well, men who'd probably not heard grapevine dispatches that Sanders and Brandon were a pair.

"What's going on?" I asked.

One of them said, "Joe Sanders had a massive heart attack."

The floor fell away. I put a hand on the wall but recovered before they noticed. "When?" I asked.

"Six o'clock this morning, at home."

The other one said, "A lot of heart attacks occur in the morning. That's why I don't do my exercises right off."

"Better just to stay in bed," the first man said, "catch a few winks."

I piled into the director's office. "What happened to Joe Sanders?"

Paul Ferris looked up, paused, and said, "He died."

"No he didn't," I said, taut as a spring.

"I'm afraid it's true. I checked at Irvine Med Center." He looked at me differently now, as if recalling that Joe and I are more than colleagues. "Why don't you take a seat, Smokey?"

"Who reported it?"

"His ex-wife. That's who they had on file."

"There's some mistake. This can't be true."

"Why don't you sit down?" Paul rose and rounded the desk to come toward me.

Fucker. Leave me alone, is what I felt. I walked away.

I drove. I parked. Several times. I cried.

On a long dirt road off Sand Canyon I sat under eucalyptus trees so tall they seemed to be the heavens. Sat there thirty minutes or so with the window down, studying rows of plants, the dry dirt beside the car, the patterns of shed leaves ranging in color from gray to wine. Above, the sky was without tone or variation. Birds flitted, but not with energy.

I fell into a spasm of hard weeping, recalling moment after moment of Joe. Joe and me, Joe and Ray, Joe and others. This man could not be gone. My heart raged against life and anyone I knew who'd slighted him, shorted him, not given everything he'd expected. I myself stood high on that list for omissions and commissions, for why hadn't I recognized the warning signs?

My throat ached. My eyes burned as if I'd walked through smoke. The flesh of my face had a quivering life of its own.

Within minutes of reaching home, I had a call from Joe's son. We cried, recovered, cried again. I asked if he was going to be okay. He said yes, yes, but there was one thing. Then all I heard were sobs. "David, where are you? Are you at home?"

"I'm not at my apartment."

"Your mom's?"

"No."

"Where, then?"

"I'll have to call you back." He hung up.

Then one of those reprieves you see only in your trembling dreams occurred. Paul Ferris called . . . to say Joe wasn't dead.

"I've been trying to reach you," he said. "Apparently a nurse blew off her mouth when she didn't have all the facts."

My knees were weak and I sat. Joe, alive!

The director waited, then said, "You need somebody there?"

"No. No."

"So they're watching him real close now, that's all I know. If you need some time off," Paul said, "it's okay."

"Paul, I just got off the phone with his son. He still thinks his father's dead."

"His mother phoned us," he said. "She thinks you might know where he is."

"I don't. He didn't say. He's very upset."

When we hung up I grabbed my keys, flew out the door, raced down the stairs to my car. All I could think of was, "He's *alive.*"

They wouldn't let me in. I couldn't even be sure Joe would get the message I left at the nurse's station.

I fell into bed exhausted when I got back.

The next morning Joe was still in ICU. I found his Jennifer's phone number in the book under Joe's old listing and called her. We commiserated, then I asked about her son. She was worried sick: She still couldn't reach him. My heart tore for him, but there was nothing I could do. I went in to work.

A strange thing happens when the mind is under stress. There's fog, and clumsy thinking. And then, for no reason I can put a name to, sometimes there's heightened clarity.

I went to Property and checked out the belt I bagged from the Nita Estevez case. I remembered it had laced edges. Again I processed it for prints. I got nothing I could use. I examined the photos Mona had made of the Nellie Gail Doe and tried to compare the ripples across his face with what I saw on the belt before me. It couldn't be a match. The case circumstances were too different. But it was interesting: a laced belt as a binding or ligature in both these cases.

I went through my three Doe folders again to be sure I hadn't overlooked anything. At ten o'clock Dr. Schaeffer called. "I know he's not yours but I thought you might like to know the Capistrano victim got identified," she said.

"You bet."

"His relatives came looking, from the sketch in the paper. So it's a small victory anyway. His name was Victor Minor Montalvo. His family are field workers. One brother works in an auto-body shop, I recall. A girlfriend did the fancy haircut for him," she said.

On a yellow pad I wrote down *Victor Minor Montalvo,* set a dash, wrote *Capistrano,* then *Doe 4.*

"We gave him the name 'Alligator' for a while. Isn't that awful? A watch came with him with an alligator in the center. The jaws were clock hands."

I wrote *"Alligator"* on the pad. "How's Doe Three, the Turtle Rock?" I asked, and wrote on the next line *Froylan Marcos Cordillo—Turtle Rock—Doe 3.*

"Nothing new that I know of," she said. "Same for Doe Two. Same nothing. We had a group out front before the

Montalvo family came in, demanding action. Chief Yaroshak is fit to be tied."

She asked about Joe then, and I told her. Then she told me about her nephew, whose autopsy she had had to perform. He asphyxiated on a bit of a carrot his mother left in a dish on the coffee table. "She's a basket case. He had just learned to pull himself up. My brother took her to be near her family in Illinois."

"How terrible, Lenore."

"Terrible doesn't really cover it," she said. "But what can you do? You go on. Now my ex is agonized about *our* kids. He gives me the third-degree on the phone every night, drives me crazy. I tell him, Well, *you* come over and watch them if you don't trust the nanny that you and I both interviewed and hired. It's tough."

"I can imagine."

"Yikes! I've got to get going. I have to get to the preschool early today. My nanny doesn't drive."

CHAPTER 15

Joe was still out of my reach. Not being a relative, I could only get so far. "Tomorrow," the nurse said. "He could be out by then and moved to critical. Call then."

I felt helpless and anxious. Yet, it was not like with Bill. I was too young then. As many crimes and vagaries as I've seen since then, I have still also experienced reasons to hope, and so I did.

On my way home I counted 15 helicopters flying formations of staggered threes in a perfect blue sky, their speed so slow the blades seemed distinct at the ends of a center fuzz. It struck me that these lumbering birds were no less beautiful than those with feathers.

And on the banks of the bay when I took a walk late that afternoon, I saw a bird resembling a sandpiper bobbing along, except he was clunkier and all-over gray on top, not tan, though mottled like a piper. I couldn't place it and vowed to look it up.

I watched a covey of coots zero between mallards and snatch food directly from the ducks' mouths. How greedy, how unsatisfied, we all are.

Back home I took out a leftover sandwich and radishes trimmed but pale as corpses, and milk. I set out a bowl for Motorboat, who planted his forefeet on the rim and waited for me to get the bag of feed, his nose high in the air and twitching. The two of us chewed while I stood at the sink and looked out the window at the bay. Below an intense orange sky the mud flats gleamed. I could see a group of plovers and godwits and the gray bird I'd seen earlier and couldn't name.

My *Peterson's Guide* was on the end of the counter. I paged through it to check the outline of the bird I couldn't identify. I went to get my field glasses from the other room and returned to spy on the bird. Smaller than a whimbrel, fatter than a lesser yellowlegs. Finally I came upon it: a wandering tattler. Strictly speaking, out of his territory. I rolled the name over in my mind, its sound reminding me of Dave Sanders, his concern about betraying his roommate, about *tattling.* I wondered how he was holding up, this new thing with his father.

I set the book down and reached to stroke Motorboat's head. He stopped eating, just raised his head to my hand and let his little buck teeth hang down as his mouth fell open. I couldn't solve the Does and I couldn't fix Joe, but maybe I was good for something.

A little while later I was in the living room finishing off a celery stick and watching TV. I saw Gil Vanderman's business card on the end table and picked it up. Muted the TV. And I don't know why, but I pulled the phone toward me and punched in his number. I would just let it ring twice. But he picked up.

"Hi. This is Smokey Brandon."

"Hey!"

"I thought I'd call."

"Great to hear from you," Gil said.

"Well, I don't have anything to say, I just—"

"I would've called *you* but I don't have your number. I guess you didn't throw away my card. How've you been? Want to go grab a coffee?" His voice was rich but quick and vibrant.

I said, "Probably not tonight."

"When's a *good* night? Oh, wow! You know what I just saw fly by here?"

"What?"

"An owl with a rat in his talons. He flew right by my patio."

"Neat," I said.

"Say, you know how I said I'd seen you before? Well, you've probably seen me, only you didn't know it. I give classes for kids down at the bay. Ever see us, spread out on blue tarps down there? Sure you have."

"Maybe so." I had, as a matter of fact.

"So when's a good night for dinner?"

"Actually, I don't know if—"

"How's tomorrow night?"

"Weekdays are not usually good."

"What kind of work do you do? I mean, where's your office? I could meet you."

"I work for the county. Santa Ana."

"Gee, that's too bad."

"Why do you say that?"

"The whole city's a Nine-One-One," he said.

"Come now. It's not that bad."

I took the phone with me to check on Motorboat. Guinea pigs don't jump, so I could have left him on the counter, but I picked him up and took him to be with me on the couch. Soon he'd try to take a chomp of the fabric, and I'd have to put him back.

"What do you do there for the county?" Gil said.

"Check on people."

"Social worker? Parole officer, like that?"

"Something like that."

"Any rate," Gil said, "maybe I could meet you wherever."

"Gil, you know what? I probably shouldn't have called, really."

"What, you don't eat lunch?"

"I eat lunch. It's just—"

"Good. I hate those women always worried about eating/not-eating. They can't just relax and enjoy life. Like, what'd you have tonight? It'll tell me something about you."

"I don't really think you care what I ate tonight, Gil, and if you did I'd worry about you."

"So what about tomorrow night? Is that good?"

"You know what? I really didn't . . . The thing is, I'm going with someone."

"So? Two bird-nerds doing lunch, what's the harm. But if you want to just yak on the phone, I'm okay with that."

"Thanks, Gil." But in a little while he invited me to Harbor Island to see great blue herons in their huge nests at the top of pine trees. He said his folks lived there. We could have dinner.

"That's terrific, Gil, but I don't think so."

"Mom's a great cook. We'll go down to Balboa. A friend of mine lets me use his boat. We're across the water in ten minutes. How's Sunday?"

He was so persistent I couldn't help but laugh. "Gil? Don't count on it, really. A lot is going on in my life."

"Oh. No problem. But you'll like the herons. Of course, we have the garden-variety pelicans out there too, and—"

"That's okay, Gil."

"Remember, it wouldn't be a date or like that."

"Herons," I said.

"Exactly. Will you consider it and let me know later?"

"I guess so."

"You know, that first day? I said to myself, 'Anybody named Smokey's got be all right'."

"You're a little over the top, Gil."

"Yeah, but to know me is to love me."

Pig was asleep on my stomach, warm as a new pancake. Such trust. I flicked a wrist and un-muted the TV and put it on to a VH station. I closed my eyes. Images came but this time not the brutal images of death, but of birds, their forms, behavior, and beauty.

Soon a song came on: "Baby, I Need Your Lovin'."

I remembered a night that followed a day so steamy the bushes were chasing the dogs around. All the coolers seemed to be gasping. There was a club in North Vegas this side of seedy. That night . . .

My costume was colored the kind of pink you find in the well of a rose or the back of a baby's mouth. A reckless pink, an Indian pink: the costume—what there was of it. Heels, rose-colored and very high, with thin straps crossed way up the ankle.

I'd been drinking whisky backstage with the other girls. I took right to whisky the first time I tried it: loved the scent, taste, the effects. No reason to be surprised. That's what it's designed for.

There was a dancer named Linda who went by Lacey. I wasn't that drunk. *She,* however, was gone. She took an ice cube from her drink. "Here, Smokey, rub this on! Got to make those little soldiers stand at attention." Her 5-year-old daughter was there, cutting paper-dolls out of a book, but badly.

I said she was stone-assed wicked and told another woman to cover little Julie's eyes. I'm not proud of any of that, but that was the way it was. I knew I was coming to the end of my stay at Foxland. Perhaps that's why I let myself get more than a little tipsy. I didn't know where I would go, just knew it was almost over. I remember thinking maybe I'd use Julie's scissors to snip off a red snake of hair and give it to somebody sweet as a goodbye gift.

When it was my turn on stage, through the dim light I saw a man and his son I'd conversed with several times before. A good dad, bringing the son to distract him from recent widowhood. Every once in a while the son (his name was Donny) would thrust his fist into the air and cry, "Roll with it, bay-bay!" and "Rock it on down!"

A hat. I had an enormous black velvet hat. Where did it go? I paid a hundred dollars for it, if you can imagine. Almost a week's wages. Extravagant in every way. A long, wide, soft, hat. You can leave your hat on. I remembered a thick-necked guy with a hoarse voice yelling, "Give you every *inch* of my love!"

One time the son was there without the father but with friends. At my break they called me over. One of them said, "Can I dance with you, can I wash your feet, can I wash your hair?" Can I wash your *hair?* I'd forgotten about that till now. The originality of it. The silliness of it. I confess, I was tempted.

Any woman is four or five women, the writer said.

That final night I went home with the father, but I remembered the son. Tan, blond, good shoulders—a lot like a younger Gil Vanderman, but a wilder look in the eyes. I wondered whatever became of him. "Rock it on, bay-bay! Do it up right!"

I saw the father once afterward in a grocery store, but not the son. Donny, he said, was up north fighting fires. Maybe now, these days, like Gil he's out teaching kids about birds. Flamingos. Pink ones. Or helping a little girl cut out dolls, badly.

CHAPTER 16

A BOCA DE JARRO: This was the headline strung over the sketches of Doe #1 from Technology Park, Doe #2, the Nellie Gail. The Turtle Rock, #3, now known as Froylan Marcos Estancio Cordillo. Victor Minor Montalvo, the one with the good haircut, in the water near the river cane. The words appeared on the front page of a Spanish-language newspaper now smack in the middle of a conference table at sheriff's headquarters: *A BOCA DE JARRO:* AT VERY CLOSE RANGE.

Boyd Russell had doughnuts on the table, and an insulated pitcher of coffee, when I came in. Will Bright arrived and lay his folders next to ours. Piece by piece, we went over everything we had: photos, sketches, ballistics reports; diagrams, lists, printouts, hand-drawn maps. "Let's have the newspapers run the sketch for Doe One again," I said.

"We can do that," Boyd said.

"That leaves the first one," Will said, "and case 00-6272DC, Nellie Gail. Two ID'd, four unsolved."

"I ran those receipts from the wallet back to the store," Boyd said, flicking his eyes up at me because it had been my suggestion in the first place. "Nobody remembered him. Zero on this one."

And so it went.

That noon I took Joe flowers. The nurses wouldn't put them in his room. I left them at the desk, where he had a view from his room, and just stepped inside the doorway. He

111

looked wan and tired even in his sleep. A clear plastic tube ran under his nose and another into his left arm. "What am I going to do with you?" I quietly asked his sleeping form.

His son at least now knew Joe was alive and was in fact improving. Jennifer phoned and told me that. Her voice was tight as a bow string. David still would not come home.

I wasn't done with flowers. On my way to my car I stole two daffodils for Trudy from around the fountain in the common area. I put them on her desk in a plastic sports bottle I found in her wastebasket and wondered if she'd see them before she left.

I saw her in the hallway later. She said, "I got your flowers. Thanks, but you don't have to keep doing that."

"It's no problem."

"Well, you don't have to, really. I mean, the thing is, I'm allergic. I gave them to the receptionist." We laughed.

I said, "Listen, Homicide would like another sketch of the Doe from Nellie Gail. Could you do that?"

She said, "I didn't do that one very well."

"Nobody's criticizing you."

"I knew it when I did it," she said.

"You had things on your mind."

"I'll have it tomorrow."

When I left, I patted her arm and later hoped that wasn't a lame, condescending, or pitying thing to do.

Fifteen minutes before quitting time, Joe called. "Hey," I said, "are you supposed to be making phone calls?"

"I'm going nuts in here," he said. "Vega just got off the phone or I'd be ready to call it quits."

"I'll be down to keep you company."

"Better not. I'm going in for more tests in a while."

"This late? More tests?"

"Nothing serious, don't worry."

"What time should I come? Around dinner?"

"Don't come tonight, babe, if you don't mind. Dave's coming. I'd like a little time alone with him."

"Tell him I said hello."

"I guess he's been pretty upset. Guess I'll have to get my rear in gear and get outta here, huh?"

"How poetic. That rhymes."

"I been thinking of growing a beard, getting a beret."

"Today's poets shave their heads, pierce their nipples, and get tattoos."

"Guess I'll skip that, then," he said.

Saturday morning, when I saw him around nine, he was asleep again. He looked no better than before and now his cheeks were as fiery red as makeup on a daft woman.

When his eyes opened, he said, "Hi, Sourpuss." I knelt beside him. He stroked my hair. I gave way for a moment with tears.

"Hey, who's the patient here?" he said.

Seating myself back in the chair, I said, "I'm a jerk," and wiped away a tear. "You're looking great," I lied. "How do you feel?"

"Punctured, pinched, molested, mad as hell."

"You're supposed to be calm. Want those blinds open more?"

"Leave them," he said, and pointed to a partition behind which lay another patient.

"I miss you, you rotter."

He folded the top edge of his sheet. Smiling, he said, "I had a dream. Like Martin Luther King."

"A dream?"

"I was free." He cut his eyes over to me. "I could fly." The telephones were ringing softly at the nurses' station. I heard his room companion whose every breath ended with a little whimper, the water dripping in the lavatory, the hum of fluorescent lights, the random clicking of machines next to Joe with green, red, and amber pixels glowing. "I messed up, Smokes," he said.

"Healthy eating, more exercise from now on," I said.

"Might as well kill me now."

I stroked his legs. "I brought you flowers. They're out at the desk."

He gave me an imaginary kiss. "How are things at the lab?"

"Peachy keen. You don't need to know what's new at work."

"I suppose everybody's standing around talking about me and not doing diddly worth of work."

"Hah. They were bidding for your parking space."

He smiled and closed his eyes. I looked around to see if any nurse was about to tell me I'd overstayed my time. Then his gaze was on me. "This old man's screwed up your life, hasn't he?"

"They need to give you juice for your head in that tube," I said.

"You should be hanging out with guys zonked on pro football. Not sick old fuckers like me."

"I should go, let you rest. How 'bout I sneak you in some booze and pizza later?"

"Baby?" He gave two pats on the bed, and I sat. He said, "Don't change." I bent to kiss him. "You smell great," he said.

"You smell like Lysol."

"Latest fashion aroma. Take care of yourself," he said.

"Me," I said.

"Yeah."

"Want water? A cloth? A . . . a . . ."

"Nothing. Get outta here." I stood, wanting to think of something more I could do.

Then he said, "I should've ID'ed him right off. I've beaten him before. I'll beat the sucker again."

A few steps away I turned mid-step to a low wolf-whistle; looked back once more just as Joe edged his chin away and shut his eyes. I could still see the smile.

Jennifer Sanders was outside the elevator when I reached the first floor. She said she'd like to talk, so we went to the basement cafeteria and had coffee at one of those shiny Formica tables whose legs can never find the floor all at the same time.

She was a brunette with a tender translucence to her skin.

"David says he's got a new apartment," she said, "but he didn't give me his number and I forgot to ask." She reached beneath the table to get her purse, and pulled out a pack of Virginia Slims. "I know. Nobody smokes anymore. They'll probably throw me out of here," she said, looking around.

"We can go outside," I said.

"Maybe we better."

She got up, tucking the cigarettes back in her purse but keeping the unlighted one tucked in her palm. "Joe used to hate it, my smoking," she said, with a nervous smile. "Even though he did at one time." She offered me one, and I shook my head no.

A tunnel led to the street. Outside, she lit up and drew in a long breath and exhaled upward into the limbs of a bottlebrush tree whose trunk was a raceway for ants.

I saw the Nellie Gail, the ants making their curved way around Juan Doe Number Two.

"I have to go to work pretty soon," she said. "Real estate is weekends and nights, a hazard of the profession."

"I remember now, you're in real estate." I felt funny talking with the ex-wife of my lover, revealing in even the slightest that she'd been the topic of any conversation between Joe and me.

Perhaps she felt it too, because she said, "Listen, I, uh, know this is awkward. But you don't have anything to worry about." She drew in another long hit. "You had nothing to do with Joe and me, I know that. If it wasn't now, it'd be then. If it wasn't then, it'd be now. It was a long time coming."

"Thanks for saying so."

"I want to ask you a favor." She massaged her elbows, cigarette intact. "If my son comes to you, do your best for him."

"Of course. But I can't see him doing much of that."

"David and I have been close, closer than he's been with his father really, except this last year or so. It might be because of college, the need to break away. Each of us has to do it, sometime in our life. Now this, with his father. It might be too much. Maybe now's the time when David needs to draw to another adult."

"I'm sure he'll always need his mother."

She cut her eyes at me. "Don't patronize me."

"I didn't mean it to sound that way."

"David likes you," she said, and took another quick hit off her cigarette. Then she reached forward to stub it out on the tree trunk, not noticing she'd caused a catastrophe on the ant speedway. "The senior and the junior mother figure," she said. "Is that a cruel thing to do to a boy, or what, two mother figures?"

I smiled, and just as I started toward her to give her a consoling embrace she saw it coming and turned away and tugged open the door against the air conditioner suck.

Mrs. Langston knocked on my door about five. She'd

come over to borrow sugar, honest to God, just as neighbors used to in the good old days. She heard my guinea pig whistle and looked in the laundry room and said, "That's the cutest thing I've ever seen."

"They eat these little guys in South America," I said.

"No! How could they?" Mary said, now brave enough to lean forward and push a forefinger over its head between the ears. He let his mouth drop open, showing his tiny bucked teeth. "I gave up consuming anything with a face some time back," Mrs. Langston said. "I thought if I just age veggies it would change my arthritis. It didn't, but what the heck. How's your friend Joe?"

"He's better."

Her face drew down, then she said, "I lost one husband to a stroke, another to a heart attack."

"I'm sorry."

"They were good men, too." Her face brightened. "My third husband, he was a kick in the head. Always kept me laughing. Kept other women happy, too. Him, I *gave* a heart attack." Her eyes fairly sparkled. "How're we coming on the Does?"

Does. Because of me she was using the language.

"Not very far, not very fast," I said.

"Well now. You all better get with the program, huh?"

"I'll see to it we do that," I said as she turned to go.

"You *do* have some fun once in a while, don't you?" Her head was cocked like Columbo just before he asks the last question that will lead to the killer's confession. "Because if you don't," she said, "you'll regret it one day. Remember that." She shook a warning finger. "Listen to one who knows," she said earnestly before she shut the door.

117

CHAPTER 17

"How's that old ticker today?"

"Quiet as a horse-thief after a hanging."

"Why doesn't that answer sound as good as it should?"

"Listen, do me a favor tomorrow?"

"Of course," I said.

"Get in touch with Harold Raimey. Ask if he can check the trunk of the husband's car, will you? I know he'd need another warrant, but it'd sure be nice if hubby had some old tennis shoes stuffed in a gym bag back there that match our shoe impressions on the plywood."

"You're incorrigible, but I will. Should I drop by today?"

"Know what's weird?" Joe asked. "They tell you to cool it on the visitors, yet I'm looking at two ugly faces right now, two old colleagues from up north. They're in town for a trial, so what do they do but come bother *me*," he said. I could hear them in the background giving him a bad time. "Why don't you come after work tomorrow night," Joe said. "We'll have a game of volleyball on the beach."

Gil Vanderman. I forgot he was going to call. He told me his mother makes a fabulous asparagus salad and put the sweet-voiced woman on the line. "Hi, Smokey. This is Ivalyn."

"Nice to meet you, Ivalyn."

"Gil's father and I *would* be very pleased to have you over. The herons are something to see."

Gil was twirling a long-stemmed lily between his fingers

when I met him on the sidewalk outside a café on Balboa Island. He handed it to me as he commented on my looks, then said the bouquet of mixed flowers he held in the other hand was for his mother.

"Anyone who'd bring flowers to his mother gets my vote."

"I told you I was a good guy," he said.

He wore nutmeg wool pants and a blue chambray shirt open at the neck. A gold watchband showed at his wrist. He seemed a little nervous, and I was surprised at that. He said we'd better get going so we'd still have light.

We were underway across the channel, the water green, the Torrey pines on the island ahead cutting black shapes out of a sky still ripe with gold. Airplane lights drifted inland, while a gull curved oceanward looking for a last morsel. Gil pointed and said, "You can just make out the nests." And I could. Eight giant ones, three feet across, Gil told me.

He nosed the boat up to a small dock jutting out from a deep, tailored lawn whose grass was sprinkled with tiny white flowers. A red brick pathway ran up its middle. I was impressed. A place where dreams come to settle.

Gil's parents came out of the house and stood on the deck and waved. His mother's dark hair was swept white at the sides. She cut an elegant figure in an Indian cotton dress with a silver belt and silver sandals. Gil's father could have passed for a heavier "Crocodile Dundee."

"I've been holding out on you," Gil said. "My dad, that nice old guy up there?" he said, motioning with his head, "with the little pot belly and reading glasses? He's a retired judge. I mentioned you one time, and he recognized your name. He told me you work at the crime lab."

I felt somehow exposed. I rubbed my arms against the chill.

Mrs. Vanderman fed us shrimp scampi over rice, baked

spinach with yellow squash and parmesan, and the salad: asparagus with a creamy dressing of cilantro and lime. For dessert, lemon mousse. We talked about her work as a magazine editor, the bankrupt county, the recent fires, the earthquakes, birds, and Gil's astonishing—by his mother's words—work in photography. I acknowledged my job in the crime lab, and Gil's father spoke briefly about his life as a judge but seemed content leaving it at that.

After dinner, Gil stood by the fireplace holding his wine glass, rich fire colors lighting his hair, the wine, the glass, as soft music played. His mother served chocolates and his father offered liqueur. For a while I didn't think about murder. Or Joe. Or his anguished son.

At my car, standing there after I unlocked the door, Gil said, "Would you come back to my place, Smokey?" He touched my cheek with the side of a finger and pressed his forehead to mine. "I have etchings," he said.

"No thanks, Gil." He was sweet and he smelled wonderful, and I'd had an evening I was grateful for. More, I was charmed. A man who brought you to his parents right off. Where did you find that any more? "Thanks for a great evening, Gil. I really appreciate it."

I got in. He immediately brought his knuckles to the glass and knocked. I rolled the window down.

"What, Gil?" I said, laughing.

"One more chance: Come back to my place?"

I brought his knuckles to my lips, kissed them, and said, "You are a wonderful person, Gil, and I am grateful to know you."

"That's a brush-off, huh?"

"I didn't say that."

There was something so earnest in his face that I smiled

and said what I knew would commit me to action I might come to regret. I was still warm from the good meal and good will and the man's own heat off his body, and I said it anyway. "Know what Marilyn Monroe used to say?"

"No idea at all."

"Sex should be like saying hello."

He said, "Hello," and leaned in and kissed me.

"Hello," I said back.

When I opened the door to my condo, only the thought of the tiny creature who never sleeps kept me from feeling the loneliness of the condemned with a conscience; and here I hadn't even done anything yet. I hadn't followed Gil to his place, hadn't done the wild thang with him. But I knew it was only a matter of time. I told myself I was a free soul. I just wouldn't think about it for now.

Motorboat peeped. I went to him in the darkness, with only the moon's light reflecting off the walls and appliances, and raised the lid of the cage and propped it against the wall. I slid a hand under his warm belly and lifted him out, bringing him to the heat and safe hiding of my neck, letting my hair drape over him. "How you doin', baby? Did you miss me, hm?"

His whole small body purred. I hummed to match his sound, the two of us in the darkness, linked in temporary song.

That night I tossed with indecipherable dreams. I saw airplane lights in skies, and bright explosions. Upside down in the room where we found her, Little Crane hung from the ceiling.

CHAPTER 18

It was the talk of the lab. Orange County, said a senator, was in the grip of another serial killer. Heat was channeling down from the top echelons. Atop the top was this senator with a Z-ending to his last name and a Hispanic look to his features—I saw him on the news before leaving my condo.

I had two messages on my voicemail from reporters. At last they had more than mega-deals to moon over and Presidential peccadilloes at which to snicker, but unless I wanted to be picking up early retirement forms, those calls had to go unanswered.

What had I missed in evidence collection? There was so little to go on. Current wisdom says most serial killers are Caucasian who target Caucasians. Maybe we had one out of type: Such was the case in Atlanta, that killer of black kids.

I hated how psychological profilers always said these vicious morons were highly intelligent. Go ahead, give the sick fucks more glamour to feed their perverted egos. That kind of press, someone might even be inspired to try the game. Sickfuck monkey see, sick-fuck monkey do. Murder is an equal opportunity employer.

Stu Hollings had me come see him at eight and kept me till nine. Lots of talk, no result except me in a sweat from the grilling.

I was late to hook up with Bob Hammerly on a training video. Then in the afternoon I went on an arson call; no human casualties, but a stinky, tedious job nonetheless. I didn't get home until eight. Phoned Joe. He said it was all right, he was hitting the rack, I could come see him to-morrow. If anyone understood, he did.

Five minutes later, Dave Sanders showed at my door, haggard and unshaven. He had found my address at Joe's.

I brought him a can of cherry soda and sat on the arm of the couch, while he took the wicker chair near the glass slider.

"What's cookin'?" I said gently. "You don't look so great."

He took a moment, then said, "Dad's going to die, isn't he?"

"David."

"He is."

"Well, then, we're all going to die," I said.

"Before his time," he said.

"Whenever we die, it *is* our time."

"You believe in predestination then?"

"I think we kid ourselves a lot. I believe we have both more control and less control over our lives than we think we do."

"So in your mind we have no chance of changing life's events."

"That's not exactly it," I said. "I think sometimes we can."

"Predestination is like nihilism, isn't it? Nothing matters."

"I believe in fate," I said. "At least, that's what we say when we don't know what else to say." I laughed, trying to take some of the weight off of the subject.

His face stayed locked in seriousness.

"What I don't believe in," I said, "is Somebody-Up-There directing traffic. A lot of people do. I don't knock it. Whatever works. Are you concerned for your father's spiritual state?"

"I'm concerned about my own!"

"Then I'm not the one you need to be talking to," I said.

His eyes threaded with red. "Someone's going to be hurt,

maybe even killed, and I can't stop it, and I don't know what to do!" Tears sparkled. Saliva bunched in his mouth.

The divorce, the stresses of college, his father's brush with death: the kid had cracked. I went into the kitchen and got a clean dishtowel, ran it under the faucet, and brought it back to him. "Here," I said.

"My roommate . . . I told you about him."

"Yes. He steals."

"Put a nickel on the nightstand, it's in his bank the next day. He'd steal his grandma's dentures if he could." His voice was harsh, a serrated knife through cardboard. "I didn't tell you *what* he steals."

"Software off the internet."

"*And* hardware. He helps guys get jobs in computer companies, then tells them what parts to steal. He fakes their resumes, pretends he's a reference if someone calls. The parts, he keeps or sells, pays a commission."

"Have you tried to stop him?"

"What we're talking here is a guy with no guts," he said, jabbing his thumb into his chest. "A guy without an ounce of integrity or guts."

"That's a little harsh, don't you think?" I wished I had his father to deal with this. Even his mother. What did I know about twenty year olds? "For pete's sake, what is so terrible about you?" His face bunched, and I thought he was going to break down again so I said, "Tell me more about this roommate. Greg's his name?"

"Greg Cheng. Cheng with his little *bidness*," he said.

"Are other students involved with him?"

"It's not the money most of the time. It's for kicks, power. I was brought up . . . I mean, you have these ideals. . . ."

"Are *you* involved, David?"

"No!"

"I'm just trying to understand," I said.

"He's got this network, like Fabian. Trainees."

"You mean Fagin?" I said.

"What?"

"From *Oliver Twist*. It was Fagin who taught the pick-pockets."

"Yeah, jeez! See? I'm off my beam. Fabian," he said in disgust. "The other day someone asked my middle name. I had to stop and think," he said, shaking his head. "So fucked."

"You said someone was going to be harmed," I said.

The room was so quiet I thought I heard a Daddy Longlegs spider in the corner crawling. Then: "I can't be sure. But. . . ."

"Why would you say that if you didn't think it was true?"

"I said I can't be *sure*." He stood and paced the room, then went to the slider and opened it.

Out on the patio, a sparrow that should have been asleep dripped a white mess down a green plastic chair, then tilted her head at what wondrous work she'd wrought and flew off.

David went out and stood at the railing of the balcony. I followed. He pointed over the bay. "I've been sleeping in the bushes," David said. "In something like that."

"The bushes?"

"Little grass shack by the railroad track in Hono-loo Hawaii. There's a wash along La Paz goes for miles. There's this real tall pampas grass there. Cheap, very cheap. Stars at night, big and bright, deep in the heart of Orange County."

"What in the world are you talking about, David?"

His eyes shone like those of a man trapped in the rage of grief, a man who always thought *he'd* be the first to go yet saw his family stripped off one by one. Then he said, "You don't know me. You don't know me at all."

No argument there, I was thinking. Is the son the father,

the father the son? Joe is low-key.

David . . . who knew?

"I'd like to."

"You don't know if what I say is a crock or not."

"Well, you got me there," I said. "Did you ever think of talking about this with your mom, David?"

"She'd freak."

"Sometimes parents can take a lot more than—"

"You don't know *her* either. She tried to commit suicide once. Did you know that? Did Dad tell you that?"

"No."

"That's right. He wouldn't. Because things don't go wrong in a family like ours, see. Crime lab, D.A., cop. Same thing."

"David," I said. "You need to go home. Your mother needs you. You need your mother."

"I can't go home. Did I get *that* right? Thomas Wolfe, 'You can't go home again'? I'm an English major. So I thought. Or did Fagin say that? I forget."

His dramatics were getting to me. "Look," I said, "we can Play-Me-A-Riddle all day. You came here because you needed to talk. I'm here, I'm listening. So talk." Then I added what I shouldn't have: "Or don't waste my time."

He bent his head to look at the muddy toe of his sneaker propped on the lower rail. A pained or an arrogant smile pulled across his lips. Then he was into the house and striding through the living room and out the front door.

He had the leg length over me; I couldn't keep up. I chugged over to my car and dug the extra key out from under the fender and followed him down Bay Drive, catching up to him and talking to him through my open window.

"Dave, I'm an idiot. Get in the car. For your dad's sake."

That slowed him down.

"He needs you. He needs you to be okay. Come on. We can take a drive. If you don't want to talk, you don't have to. You want to, I'm all ears."

I thought I'd lost. Then he veered and crossed the street to me.

We drove down Pacific Coast Highway to a place I knew where we could sit on a rock wall high above the sand and watch the surf. On the way, I tried engaging him in talk about beach clean-ups and hotel development on the hillsides and volleyball in the sand, but it wasn't until we sat on the wall with a soda and onion rings from a drive-thru and watched the ocean exploding in white froth against a blue velvet night that he began to relax.

"Are you ready now?" I finally asked.

Below, a rush of surf raced forward, and beneath the noise I heard him say: "Someone has been murdered." He glanced at me, then squeezed his eyes shut.

I let him gather himself . . . as I was doing the same.

"His name was Freddie. He wasn't a student. He was somebody Greg Cheng knew. I think Greg either killed him or had him killed. He's a fucking Mafia all to himself. He's evil. Evil!"

A wave eased forward to capture a twist of paper on the sand below and suck it into its maw.

"David," I said cautiously, "if this is so, we have to—"

"*If* this is so? It's *so!*"

"Has he threatened you?"

"He doesn't have to."

"Why didn't you tell your father?"

"Did you forget? He's in the hospital!"

"But before. You could have told him before."

127

"You tell yourself you're not seeing what you're seeing. You tell yourself you're crazy, nobody's *that* bad. You've seen too many DeNiro movies. Maybe I'd just heard too many fantastic stories from Dad and his friends. Then again, maybe I didn't *want* to know," he said angrily. "David, Gutless Wonder."

"Stop," I said, and touched his arm. "It's not your fault."

"One day I borrowed Greg's computer when he wasn't there. Mine was acting up. I didn't know the program I was using very well. I brought up one of Greg's files, like, a chart. I was going to just make a copy of it and change all the data for my project. That way I wouldn't have to set up all the fields myself, you know?"

"Right."

"So I'm in there, I see all these listings for computer parts. He's got these headings: *Part Number, Description, Supplier. Distribution,* a column for that. In *Supplier* and *Distribution* he's got these initials, people I know, or some of them. There's Freddie—F.M.C.—and Izzy." He said the last name with contempt.

"Izzy's he just wrote 'Izzy' for. That's why I paid attention at all, because of Izzy's name. I'd heard Greg talk to him on the phone. So then I pay more attention to what's in the database. I look in the last column. I had to scroll over, you know, to the right because it all didn't fit on the screen. He's got dollar amounts there. It was, like, 'Page one of thirty-four.' All this money, sub-totaled on every page. We're talking money here. This is the hardware, not the software. The software, man, that alone. . . ."

"Did you see the final amount?"

"I paged down, two, three of them, then Greg comes home. I start to tell him what's up, me using his computer, and he flies into this *rage.* I mean, I thought he was gonna trash me right then and there. He had me up against the *wall*. Little guy, he's not that big, not that strong, but I thought I'd had it. I stayed out of his way for two days."

The waves were huskier now and nearly reaching the foot of the stairs below.

"About the murder . . ." I said.

"I'm getting there," he said. "Can we go in? It's cold. . . ."

"Good idea."

We got back in the car. I didn't start the engine.

"I don't know details," he said. "I just know they happened."

"Tell me, best you can."

"What I'm going to say *now* is that I don't *know* he had anything to do with it, okay?, but I *know*."

"Oh David."

"See?" He turned to me, emotion twisting his face.

"Wait. I believe you, okay? Let's go from there."

"So things kind of got back to normal. Exams were coming up, winter break. Jason . . . I forgot to tell you . . . we used to have another roommate, a guy named Jason. Jason had sense. He never came back from break. He asked me to send him a box of his stuff, and I did. *He* wasn't involved, I know that."

"You mentioned the name Freddie."

David took a deep breath, then said, "I saw him in the cafeteria one time and once in our apartment. Happy guy, neat guy. I asked him, 'What's your major?' He says, 'Huh?' I says, 'Major, major.' Greg says 'Freddie's major is pussy,' and laughs." David threw me a glance and said, "Sorry."

"That's all right."

"He wasn't a student, I found out later."

"And you think he's dead."

"There was a sketch in the paper last week."

What he told me next was the name: Freddie Cordillo. The Turtle Rock Doe.

He phoned his father the night he saw the picture. He knew it was Freddie but just couldn't tell his dad. Then Joe had his heart attack and David knew he would never tell him.

I said, "It's a long way from stealing things, David, to murder."

"Is it? You don't know. You just don't know."

"Who else is going to be hurt?" I asked. "You said. . . ."

He shook his head and looked out the window on his side.

I started the engine and slowly pulled away. David put his head back on the headrest and promptly fell asleep, or seemed to. This boy was in deep waters, and I didn't know what to make of it.

Back home, I offered to let him stay on the sofa and he took me up on it. I lay awake knowing I should go to one of the investigators promptly. I'd never lain down on a case before. But I decided for once the dead could wait. The living needed taking care of.

In the morning, David sat in his undershirt with the sheet and blanket curled over his shorts and his bare legs hanging out. "I'm not a morning person," he said, when I handed him a glass of orange juice.

A few moments later I said, "What do you want to do about this, David?" He knew what I meant.

"Give me a little more time."

"I'm afraid if I let you think about it, you won't come."

He said, "Maybe I'd like to come around ten, if that's all right."

"Are you somebody who keeps his word?"

"If I say I'll be there at ten, I will," he said, no annoyance in his voice. He nodded toward the TV and asked, "What's on the news?"

Okay, he's had enough for now, I thought, tossing him the remote.

When I was out of the shower, I could hear a cartoon channel on. Big kid still on the couch probably, mouth open, propped on an elbow like his dad. "Is that Taz cartoons you have on?" I shouted from the bedroom. "Or doesn't he come on till afternoon?"

I toweled my hair, slipped underwear on, jockeyed through the closet to find some slacks and a blouse I liked, and blew-dry my hair for about 30 seconds, then got a funny feeling. I walked barefooted to the living room.

He had scooted.

CHAPTER 19

Nearly 500 people have died from hypothermia and sunstroke in the last seven years while crossing the border from the south, and that's not to mention drownings and other casualties. That's what a U.N. Special Envoy for Immigration Issues was saying on his sound bite that morning.

Yes, yes, but does that have anything to do with our Juan Does? What would ol' Stu have waiting for me today when I got into the lab?

And now there was David. He knew one of them, even if slightly. When I left the house, the empty orange juice glass with pulpy flakes clinging inside was on the counter with a paper towel under it and the word "THANKS" printed on it in blue ball-point. I felt a little responsible for David, yet was also locked in indecision. I'd call his mother, that's what I'd do, soon as I got to the lab.

I rolled a plastic bloodshot eyeball around on my desk while dialing numbers to find out which real estate firm she worked for. The eye's green iris wobbled within the sphere.

"He's home," she said when I finally reached her. "Sleeping. I know you put him up last night. Thanks."

"You're welcome," I said.

Her voice was modulated but I could sense the tension in it. I heard her puffing a cigarette. "He's just had it with that roommate," she said. "He's been bouncing between friends' apartments. Now he can stay with me. He says he doesn't want to bother me. Bother me? How can you raise a kid his whole life and then have him say something like that?"

"I guess they feel once they move out, they're out."

"The only revenge for parents is that the kids will get *theirs* someday, right?" she said with a nervous laugh.

"I suppose that's true."

"I'm going to urge him not to take so many classes next term. I think that's a contributor. He's so stressed. And now this with his father. You don't have any children, do you? I mean, if you did, they wouldn't be old enough for this type of thing, I mean."

"I don't have any children, no."

"I thought that's what Joe said. I couldn't remember."

"No, I don't have any."

"They can break your heart. I guess that's a cliché. But it's true, definitely true. Oh, there's my other line."

"Go ahead."

"No, the light went off," she said. "What were you saying?"

"Your son seems like a terrific kid, Jennifer."

"Oh, oh yes, he is. I didn't mean *that*. Unless you have one of your own though, there is no way you can really understand. Children can just drive—"

"When you talk to him, Jennifer?"

"Yes?"

"I think I'd be listening real hard between the lines."

"What are you telling me?"

"Just, he needs you."

"Okay-y-y. Nothing more than that?"

"I think I'd just be real open to him."

"He's told you something. What is it?"

"He . . . he's just real confused."

"As if he's the only one. That's the thing about kids. No one else has any problems. They are so completely self-

133

absorbed. David is not usually like that, but it can come out sometimes."

"I see."

"Thanks for calling. We'll be all right. If I can repay you in any way. . . ."

"Don't worry about it. Take it easy now."

"I might see you at the hospital," she said. Her voice trailed off. "I don't know when exactly."

"I hope so, Jennifer. Take care."

David had his father's looks and his mother's high-octane emotions. I sat thinking about how David looked as he pleaded to be believed, his hair too cute-curly for a grown man and too flecked with gray for a young one, his eyes too stricken for anyone.

The eyeball on my desk bumped against the taxidermy book I had not yet brought back to the basement library. I can't say why I took that book out to begin with, except that most of us here are just of the curious sort. The last thing I looked at was a chart of glass eyes for installing in the heads of critters. Gruesome, in a way, but at least these creatures had a type of immortality. For the anonymous victims of homicide there were no reminders of their time on earth at all. It was as if they had never been.

The closed folder for Froylan Cordillo was on my desk also. I sent the wobbly eye over to it. How would Jennifer feel, I wondered, getting a call from homicide investigators wanting to speak to her son? Lost in my moral quandary, I delayed picking up the phone to do what I knew I should. Again I flicked the plastic eyeball and watched it roll and shudder.

A forensic tech named Mitchell came into the bullpen where we have our desks, carrying a soft drink and a sheaf of papers. He sat sideways to his desk and put his feet up on a chair. He lipped a pencil fiercely as he studied a photo.

"Mitchell," I said.

"Whassup?" His ponytail caught between his neck and collar as he swung his legs down and reached for a stapler.

"You've heard about all those Doe cases lately?"

"Yeah, a couple. Irvine, right? Sounds serial to me."

"Sanders thinks it doesn't exactly fit a serial."

"Yeah? How's he doing, by the way?"

"Pretty good. I saw him yesterday. I'll see him again tonight."

"Bummer-and-a-half," Mitchell said.

"Yep," I said. "What are you working on?"

He leaned his steno chair back to rock on its spring tension. "Vietnamese guy capped his girlfriend and little girl. Males kill daughters more than sons, females kill sons more than daughters. That's what the new D.O.J. stats say. Wild."

"Isn't it?" I said flatly.

"Hey, now that I think of it, I believe there was a Doe found at the end of Sand Canyon yesterday."

"He's not a Doe," I said. "Believe me, I checked."

"Well, if I can help, give a yell. Hey, you see Joe, greetings from me."

"I'll tell him."

"Tell him I heard he's so hard on the nurses they went out and bought him a Get-Well card."

I went downstairs to put the taxidermy book back on the shelf. From behind a rack of books came Trudy Kunitz. Dangling from her ears were two enormous blue hockey pucks with *Mighty Ducks* lettered in white. I mentioned them.

"I decided: Dress happy, Be happy," she said. "Now, how do you like these?" She pointed a boot toe at me after lifting a long black soft-cotton skirt. They were red.

"Enough to borrow," I said.

"Nothing doing." She lowered her voice. "By the way, you'll be happy to know I have found a place, a spa, where they do holistic health for people like me. Herbs and things. Meditation."

"Trude, are you sure this is where you should be going?"

A frown sped over her face. Then she looked at me with tight, earnest eyes, and said, "Help me think positive, Smokey."

Someone coming down the stairs called her name, and she told me she'd see me later. She was off, her skirt wending its way around her legs like a mob of cats at feeding time.

I successfully avoided calling Will Bright until almost noon. When I tried, he was out. Lucky me. I stopped by Stu's to say I was going to see Joe at the hospital. He said it would be all right to be late. Not that I cared. He asked if I'd take along a block of pound cake his wife baked.

"What's that you have there?"

"Pound cake, from Stu Hollings."

"Yeah, like the doc will let me have that," Joe said.

"I know. What shall I do with it?"

"The door needs a stopper."

I glanced at his lunch tray. "You hardly ate anything. You need to eat."

"Fillet of skunk fat? No thank you."

"It can't be that bad."

"Yes it can."

"Mitchell says he heard the nurses are sending you Get-Well cards to get you out of their hair." Joe laughed at that. "King Davis told me to stick a fork in you: if you're done, get the hell back to the lab."

He laughed again, the old twinkle asserting itself in his eyes. Then he said, about David, "I put him through somethin,' didn't I?"

"Cruel and usual."

"I told him not to make a special thing of coming to see me. He's got school. . . ."

"Uh-huh."

"So. How's Mahatma Sheriff?"

"Fuhgeddaboutit. If you think you're going to get me talking about work, you're wrong."

He said to come nearer, and slipped a hand somewhere, and I laughed and told him he was well, he could sign himself out now.

Investigator Bright had just sat down in Stu Hollings' office when I walked in. I took the chair next to him.

Stu asked me, "How's the man?"

"Doing well," I said. "He said thanks for the cake."

Will had on a pearl-gray suit, white shirt, and a black tie with red and gray diamond design. His shoes were polished till they looked like plastic. He had a classy-looking black watch and a hand covered in dark hair. He may be an A-H at times, but I couldn't help appreciating the aesthetics.

With nary a preliminary, he launched in. Looking at Stu, he said, "We have an association with that rape-murder on Dresden last month and the Juan Doe at Turtle Rock."

"Dresden," Stu said. "Bombed to the ground in WW-Two."

"The Estevez case?" I said. "You're kidding."

"That one," Will said. "You and Sanders got the print ID for the Doe at Turtle Rock. . . ." He turned a sheet of paper on Stu's desk so he could read it. "Froylan Estancio Marcos

Cordillo. Cordillo was picked up for driving a stolen. He had a passenger."

"I am aware of that," I said.

"Turns out the arresting officer on the stolen wrote her name in his report: Juanita Rosa Estevez."

Stu said, "So this Cordillo knew the girl and she was a murder victim too."

"That's right, but the m.o.'s are entirely different. She was raped, strangled, and mutilated."

"It wouldn't be so unusual that these two may know each other, uh?," Stu said, "they're all of a klatch, so to speak."

"All of a klatch?" I said.

He shifted and sat up straighter and spoke louder, and said, "Well, they run into each other, they may hang on the same street corners, the same jobs, who knows?"

Will pushed his chair out to go. He said, "Well, that's it, that's all I have. But I figured you should know that. I'm over here to see Fred Singh. He around?"

"Haven't seen him," Stu said.

"Oh, and something else," he said, now looking at me. "We made Doe One. The one off Alton? Desi Cono Blanco. Went by 'Whitey,' I understand. Blanco. Means white in Spanish. Blanco didn't work at that place he had an employee badge for . . . what was it? Tri-Cycle Inc., on Marconi. The sketch did it. Anonymous tip, but the sketch did it. Your person did good. Tell him I said so."

I just nodded. I'd tell *him,* Trudy, what a good job she did.

My mind was churning slowly, but something flickered in. Joe had made a quip about Marconi while we were working prints from Doe 3, the Turtle Rock: Froylan Cordillo— Freddie. The 3-4-5-6-7 address. The phony one. So, Doe One "worked" on Marconi, and Doe Three used Marconi for a fictional residence address. How the heck did I miss that?

Well, I missed it and that was that.

And now Will was saying Doe Three knew Nita Estevez.

And I was remembering David Sanders knew Freddie.

And Freddie knew Estevez. And maybe Cordillo.

And David knew Freddie . . . and was afraid, torn, acting screwy.

And Freddie knew Estevez . . . Little Crane. . . .

"We still have a long way to go on these," Will said, at the doorway but continuing to yak. "Blanco actually worked at a computer company on Bake Parkway. No enemies as far as anyone knew, good worker, no absences."

"What kind of work did he do for them?" I said, stalling, stalling. Confused. Sick. Scared.

"Assembly. They make instruments to measure high-pressure gas used in etching computer chips. Don't ask me any more than that, because I don't know any more about that shit than that," he said with a small grin.

"Me either," Stu said, relieved.

"Well, gentlemen," I said, "I guess I have nothing to add to this discussion. Thanks, Will, for the additional information. I'll be toodling off, go try to put some sense to my notes."

"Sounds good," Will said. He turned to Stu and asked, "How are our friendly citizens' groups lately?"

"They came, they went, they vociferated. I haven't heard any more about it."

But that was about to change.

CHAPTER 20

Mitchell had a radio on when I got back to my desk. A news station cited that Sheriff-Coroner Matthew Trott met with a citizens' group called HAFARC: Hispanic-American Fairness, Action, and Respect Coalition.

HAFARC was demanding heightened action on the recent unsolved homicides of persons of apparent Hispanic origin. Sheriff Trott did his usual mouth-to-microphone attempt at resuscitation. It made me feel like crap. I left the area and paced down the hall and out the back door, then stood for a while breathing the air. A co-worker coming in from the parking lot with evidence bags asked if I was okay. "I know how it is," he said. "Some days . . . man." He gave a shake of his head and went on in.

The thing was, here was my chance to get the whole force of the sheriff-coroner's department involved . . . and I just couldn't do it. I was sandbagging; not giving over information, however remote, on these cases. But where to start? What I really needed was Dave Sanders. I needed to talk with him without alarming his mother and, most of all, Joe.

One thing I wasn't going to do was run right to Stu or even Boyd Russell. Boyd had three of the cases, Will Bright two, plus Nita Estevez. I'd go to one of them as soon as I could.

I went back in and made calls when Mitchell left the room and the other techs were off at the scopes or elsewhere. First I called Jennifer's house, hoping to find David there. Then I called her office again. She said they had lunch together and David seemed much calmer now. I told her I thought he may have left a notebook at my place; could she let him know?

"He's got a friend he wants to stay with." She sounded if she were smiling. "A girl, I'm pretty sure. Anyway, yes, I'll call him tonight."

"Wonderful. I'm glad to hear it. Listen, I'd best be getting off here. But I just wondered, did he leave a number?"

"Uh, four-seven-one-two thousand. Sounds like a business number, huh? I *guess* individuals can have the thousand numbers. I repeated it back, so I'm sure it's good."

"Thanks, Jennifer," I said. "Take care."

"I *will* do that. That is one thing I do," she said, puffing again.

It was bum. No good. When I dialed the number for David, the piercing sound of a fax tone came on.

Mitchell came back and put headphones on so he could listen to the radio without disturbing others. I felt a powerful need to talk to Ray Vega. I phoned him at home. "You're there," I said.

"Where should I be?"

"I didn't know what your shift was," I said. "Wondering if can I come talk to you tonight. About Dave Sanders."

"No prob. I'm on duty, though."

"Where will you be, say, eight o'clock?"

"Buzz me back about then. You can ride with me, help me snag some idiots. Hey, I got one for you you'll never believe. I had to go de-ghost a house yesterday."

"What?"

"This Chinese lady. She waves me down, says there's a baby crying in her house. 'Don't hurt it!', she says, 'just make it stop crying.' I go in, take a look, don't hear no baby. She says it's a ghost-baby—like I should have known. I take out my cuffs and cup 'em in my palm just so, and tell her this is

141

magic, this'll do it. I go back in. Come out. She's happy. Takes all kinds."

"It surely does, Ray. See you tonight."

Stu walked in. He glanced at Mitchell and Mitchell took his feet off the desk but didn't remove the headphones.

"Why don't I have anything on these cases?" Stu said. "I want everything you have on my desk before you leave."

"There's not that much."

"What have you been doing?"

I felt my face flush. "Stu, I've been to sixteen scenes in the last two weeks. I can't *manufacture* evidence." One toe over the line. It showed in Stu's face.

He came forward a bit and said, "I'll talk to you later," then turned and walked off.

I glanced over and saw Mitchell looking my way. "Ah, shit," I said, and went down the hall and got a stiff cup of coffee, came back and compiled an overall report for Stu, then made copies of my worksheets. I put it all in a small binder and delivered them down to Stu's office. He hated traffic and loved his wife's good cooking, so he was out the door already, which was best for both our sakes.

I was walking to the stairway of my condo when Dave Sanders appeared through a cut between two of the buildings. "Can I come up?" he asked. I'd passed his small black car at the curb on the slope below and could see it now through the cut.

"You gave your mother a wrong number," I said, when we got in. He didn't reply. "Why'd you cut out this morning?"

"I don't know."

"Sit down. Something to drink?" He nodded. I got him a Pepsi. "We have to talk, David."

"That's why I'm here," he said quietly.

"You knew Freddie Croylan."

"Barely, like I said." He rubbed a knee; then it started bouncing. The old anguish was in his eyes.

"Freddie Croylan may have known two other people murdered this past month. Did you know that? Does that make any sense to you?"

"There's someone else," he said. "Last Friday. His name was Vic Montalvo. I recognized him from the sketch in the paper, just like Freddie."

"You. . . . Was he found near Capistrano?"

"That's the one." He couldn't keep his gaze on me then, but went haltingly on with his story. Victor Montalvo had a sister. She had a friend who worked in a cantina in the heart of Santa Ana to pay off her debt to a smuggler. Her name was Nita Estevez.

I showed no emotion in my voice. "Did you know her?"

"No. But I know she died."

"I thought she worked in a garment factory."

"That was after. First she worked there, at that place. And listen to me: My roommate, Greg Cheng, he knew them all."

"David, this sounds . . . kind of over the top."

"It's not! This fucking Cheng is a fucking asshole!"

"Is he doing the killing?"

He shook his head, but I didn't know if it was to my question or for the hopelessness of the whole thing.

"He's too smart for that."

"Are you willing to talk to investigators?"

"I can't do that!"

"Why not?"

"You know why not! The reason is lying in the hospital not two miles from here."

"How would you feel about talking to Ray Vega?"

"He's a cop!"

"David, he's a friend. He can give us ideas."

I don't know quite how I did it. Maybe he was just ready. He agreed to let me phone Ray.

It took seventeen minutes to get to the station off Junipero Serra, where Ray was sitting in for a sergeant. At the front counter inside, a frowzy woman was showing her proof of insurance so she could get a towed car out. A senior citizen volunteer in a blue shirt went to get Ray. While we waited, David read the framed Certificates of Valor on the walls.

Ray came out, shook David's hand, and brought us to an office jammed with four desks, metal filing cabinets, a water cooler, metal bookcases, and footlockers. Once we were seated, Ray said, "Gotta move forward, my man. We can help."

A female officer came in and started to sit at her desk but glanced at our tight faces, asked if we needed anything, and left.

David took a deep breath, then told Ray what he told me, but added more about the sister of the victim from San Juan Creek. "Her name is Angela. She's got a friend," he said almost inaudibly. "Her friend barely speaks English. I think she's in trouble."

"How so?" Ray asked.

"Because . . . because I saw her."

"Saw her what?"

"*Saw* her." David hung his head.

"Hey, man," Ray said. "We all—"

"This girl is a slave! *Indentured*, like, to Greg Cheng and this coyote guy." He looked at me then, could read skepticism in my face. "It's true! She's supposed to pay off the

144

coyote, this lizard named Lizzaraga. He farms her out. God!"

"Easy, man," Ray said, and put a hand on David's shoulder.

"She's like a *slave* and I *used* her. And it makes me sick. *Sick.* How can I tell that to Dad, huh? What will he think of me? Worse, what will it do to *him?* I didn't know in the beginning. I thought . . . I thought she liked me." His face distorted in anguish.

"You're telling us—" Ray began, but was interrupted.

"I didn't know in the beginning. I mean, I thought it was girl/boy stuff. But it was sleazy even then. It was in this motel by the club. I wouldn't take a girl there. But I just didn't put two-and-two together. Greg and me and Vic were all at this club . . . cantina, they call it . . . and I met Vic's sister and then met *her.* Binky's her name."

"Binky?" I said.

He nodded. "Cheng wants me involved. He wanted to lure me in, get his claws in me some way. I see that now."

I got him a cup of water from the cooler.

Then he continued: "I drove up there. I was going to get her. But I don't speak Spanish and I don't know if she'd come with me and I can't make her, you know? I didn't even go in. If I blow the whistle, what happens to her? It would be like Greg to have Lizzaraga ship her back to Mexico. Or kill her, I swear. Cheng's an evil, fucking, soulless asshole, but he doesn't pull the trigger. He'd have someone else do it."

"But what's the motive?" I asked. "If he's such a good business man, why would he waste his investment."

David sagged. "Greg would order it done if he thought somebody screwed him over. Either way, I know they did it. It's illegals and theft and credit card schemes. That's what it is."

I gave Ray a glance but couldn't tell what he was thinking.

"You haven't heard the worst," David said. He raised his pained eyes to ours. "When I did find out? When I knew after a while that Lizzaraga made Binky take on guys? It didn't matter. I saw her *again*. And this time I *paid*. Knowing what was going on," he said with a miserable laugh, "I did it *again*. And I paid. I'm a *shit*. A fucking filthy shit!"

Ray touched his shoulder again. "That makes you human," Ray said. "That sure just makes you human, man."

David stared at the floor as if he found something amusing there. Then he said, "Nothing's going to stop Greg Cheng. That slime is going to rule the world."

CHAPTER 21

Ray and I stepped out into the hall for a moment, leaving David. "Okay, Vega, come up with something brilliant," I said.

He glanced over his shoulder to see if anyone was within earshot. "I say you turn this over to the investigators and quit messin' around," he said. "And we run a background on *him*," Ray said, tipping his head toward the room we just left.

"That's Joe's *son*."

"How many cops' sons you ever hear who went sideways?"

"You can't background somebody unless he's suspected of a crime. You want to lose your job?"

His tone changed and he looked at me a second and said, "You been to a fire? Either that or you been smokin' some powerful shit."

"You got it right the first time. A storage place in Costa Mesa."

"Listen, you want to go try and find this girl? That ought to cheer up our little buddy. But if she's a wetback like he says, she's gonna have to hike up her skirts and slosh back across the river, partner."

At least we'd be doing something. I said okay, let's do it.

"I have an idea."

"What's that?"

"Bring my friend Tamika along."

"You lost me there."

"Tamika can speak Spanish. I'm . . . well, not that good at it. Tamika can go with the program, is what I'm sayin'.

She's just got a way about her."

"And I don't?"

"You're a little rough around the edges."

"*What?*"

He ran right over that. "I was going to go see her tonight anyway. I'll take some vacation. Cloverfield can cover for me."

"You said you were covering for your sergeant."

"Cloverfield can handle it."

"You're something, Ray."

At the front desk a white-haired volunteer was working with a citizen who needed to know how to change his car registration over from Idaho. The man was wearing a white T-shirt with a busty woman in an orange bikini sitting on a river bank holding a fishing line, and under the picture were the words, "Bite my Lure." The volunteer was patient. The citizen was not. Ray listened to the guy tell the desk volunteer what a paradise he gave up to come to California.

"Go back to Idaho, ya pud," Ray said under his breath while he held the door open for David and me.

Ray had changed into his civvies. The three of us took off in his new blue SUV, headed for Oceanside. "What would a guy like Cheng be doing in college?" Ray asked when we were underway.

"He's very smart. He's older, twenty-nine, but he wants a degree, wants to be respectable. Then he'll have more tools *and* access to rip people off. He's from Taiwan. He was helping his parents in their computer business over there. Now he's into counterfeiting those seals, you know, that go on software boxes, to show they haven't been tampered with. Then he sells 'em, big-time. I didn't know for a long time. To tell the truth, I didn't even want to know what-all he was into. I had my own things, you know. I had . . . my life. "

Our headlights lit a reflective yellow road sign depicting a silhouette of a man, woman, and child holding hands while they run. Close to the immigration checkpoint, the signs are intended to warn drivers against people who jump from vehicles to flee across traffic lanes before Border Patrol can snare them.

We were nearing the nuclear stations at San Onofre. The twin domes gleamed softly in the moonlight like monstrous white breasts with nipple projections. Every man I've ever ridden with down this way remarked about it, except this time.

We made the turn-off to Oceanside, a mainly blue-collar town near Pendleton Marine Base. Several stores along the main street had their windows boarded up, casualties of Pentagon belt-tightening as military bases close or shrink. We parked by a chiropractor's shop with a skeleton in the window wearing a U.S. Marine cap on its yellow dome. Around the corner was the club where Tamika worked: *Roulée*. It meant "stacked," Ray said he'd been told.

Inside was dark and beery, and scattered with patrons in shavecuts. We took a table in back and ordered beer and a Coke. When the server came back we asked if Tamika was around. "Only two girls on tonight," she said. "She's next."

The one onstage wore a butch-blonde haircut and enough black eye make-up to make it look like only sockets were there. She strode around lashing a whip to the strains of "I'm a Soul Man." When it came to the part where the singer says to grab a rope and I'll tow you in, she thrust the whip-butt at a guy in the audience. I said to Ray, "You could give her your cuffs."

"Not my style," he said.

I asked David, "You okay?"

He gave a nod and looked straight ahead with no expression but rocked his Coke bottle to the music.

I hadn't told David about my unglamorous past. There was no reason to. I wondered now if I should. So I could be heard over the music I moved closer and said, "David, did your dad ever tell you I once worked in a place like this?" He looked over, trying to figure what I meant. "Not serving drinks," I said.

"No."

"Well, I did. You might guess it was a long time ago. I just want you to know sometimes you can do screwball things in your life and still find your way home."

He took it in, then looked back toward the stage. The set ended and the tough girl went behind the blue velvet curtain.

Then Tamika came on.

Some women are beautiful, and you say, yes, she's beautiful. And then there can be a row of dancers or a lineup of beauty queens, and one will stand out from all the rest. I've tried to analyze it and can't, except to say their limbs *flow*. They have muscles formed by wind. Muscles that *happen,* not those which are molded. This was Tamika.

Eyes: languid. Skin: the color, under these lights, of dark honey. Hair: to the shoulders and shiny as a grand piano.

"She's black," I whispered to Ray, when I saw her.

Cupping his hand to his mouth, he said, "I never noticed."

"It just surprised me, is all."

Ray looked at me with pride. "Mexican, Black, Irish. Her birth name is Maureen Conaty. Maureen Modesto Conaty. Tamika fits her better. Is she gorgeous or what?"

"Hollywood is cruel, I know," I said, "but here?"

She was wearing a gold sequined costume she shed within

a few bars of Sting's "I'll Be Watching You."

Be watching you. Every move you make. I gave Ray's forearm a squeeze. "Sump'n, huh?" he said.

I glanced at David, saw his appreciation but a sad distraction as well.

Every move you make.

I wished I hadn't agreed to this. I started to say so to Ray. Then Tamika removed her sequined top and let the flesh spill forth. Thick-necked marines bellowed their hearts out.

Watchin' you.

Ray let loose with a piercing whistle and Tamika flashed him a smile. The next song eased in and Tamika danced in golden spikes and G-string; and you could say nothing else, watching as she went through some of the moves I'd done when I was that limber. So long ago . . . it was me; it wasn't me.

Then the butch girl came on stage with Tamika, and they did their thing to "Money" by Pink Floyd, and the boy-marines spit blood out their eyes.

When the DJ announced a break, Ray said no to an offer of another drink by the server with the ringlets and riot-red heels, and in a moment Tamika was out, making her way to us in a violet slip-dress and straw flats. She gave Ray a peck on the cheek.

"Dynamite," Ray said.

She winked at David and me.

Ray introduced us and she reached to shake our hands, then sat down. Ray laid it out pretty quickly, how he wanted her to come with us to Santa Ana to ask around for her long lost cousin named Binky.

"I don't know, baby. I've got school tomorrow." She looked at me and David and said, "I'm in nursing school."

"How about that? Beauty *and* brains," Ray said proudly.

He said he'd have her home by twelve.

"I could do it better tomorrow night," she said.

David surprised me by saying, "This is real important, if you could." The earnestness in his face reached her.

She said, rubbing Ray's back, "I got my he-man here. What could go wrong when you got your he-man?"

CHAPTER 22

Tamika tried not to be beautiful. She dressed down, she said: black jeans and ankle boots and a turquoise tee covered by a salmon-colored denim jacket. Her hair was in a braid pulled to hover over one ear. She could pass for Amer-Indian or East Indian, Latina, Iranian, Hawaiian, or Lebanese. "So what's the plan, m'man?" she said.

It wasn't Santa Ana we went to, as it turned out, but Anaheim, in the same bleak area where a few years back an insane father with a soft voice and limpid eyes doused his son with gasoline after a day at Disneyland, set him on fire, and locked the motel room door. The nine-year-old survived but with scars that made him look like something from another world. I've seen him around town on his bike, a thin, courageous teenager now, who takes books by the armload out of the library, and I have wondered what he wants to know about the world that he doesn't already.

We found the place, *El Buho de Noche,* The Night Owl. It sat across from *El Perro Jefe,* the chief, the top dog. Its window was lit with a red neon canine wearing a gold crown.

David said, "Angela may not be there. I don't see her car. She drives an old maroon job."

"So we'll go in and find out when she does come on, okay, champ?" Ray said. "If she isn't there, we ask somebody else."

Inside, Latin music was playing. Ten or twelve customers were in the place, all men but one. The woman was seated at the bar, in her forties, smoking, one shoe hanging loose from her foot.

We took a table, and Ray, in his jeans, black shirt, and shades, scooted down so his shoulders touched the back of his chair and his legs extended under the table and out again—cool dude, he. Shortly a girl with bowed legs brought a crock of warm tortillas, butter, and frosted mugs for beer.

The doors to the kitchen opened. David gave a nod to the woman who came out and said that was Angela. She wasn't assigned to our table. When she passed by once, Ray said, "Hey, hon, come over here a minute, uh?"

"Yas?" Angela said, but stood a little away. Her dark hair had a purplish sheen and spilled around full shoulders, while an orange top revealed ample cleavage.

Ray pulled himself up, lowered his shades, and said in his becoming voice, "Come sit with us a minute?"

"You do my work, den I come sit with you." She looked at all our faces, coming back to David's often. "I get your waitress." She tooled away.

I said to Ray, "That irresistible charm."

"Next time," he said.

David said, "She'll be back." He was tense, but still managed to scarf some tortillas and butter.

Soon Angela brought a pitcher of beer. She looked at David and said, "You want somet'ing different?"

"No, I'll take the beer." He nodded toward Tamika and said, "This is Tamika. She's looking for Binky. Is she around?"

"Hi, girl. You know my cousin?" Tamika said.

Angela sent David a glance, then studied Tamika's face and flashed a frown. "Your cousin? Yeah, mine too," she said. "I got to go wait on a table." Then Angela spied the folded twenty Ray had between two fingers, held in her direction, though subtly.

She left to wait on a table but returned after saying something to our server. Standing next to Ray, her right arm was to his left beneath the table edge. He'd passed the twenty. Angela said, "Everybody happy here? You no order dinner?" She looked at Ray and dropped her voice. "You got sonthin' on your mind?"

Unsure of me, she glanced my direction a few times.

"I haven't seen my cousin since we been, like, thirteen," Tamika said in her soft, harmless way.

"Yah?" Angela said.

"Yah." Smiling, Tamika picked up the pitcher and poured for each of us as if she had all the time in the world. Looked up to say, "You think she'll come around tonight?"

"Maybe," Angela said, and started to move off.

Ray caught her by the skirt, lightly. Flirting with his voice, soft, melodious: "That *pito* over there," he said, nodding toward the man who came and went into the kitchen area, "you won't let him fire you, will you, you talkin' with us?"

"He won' fire me," Angela said. "I be back." She picked some empty bottles off another table and took them back into the kitchen. Minutes passed before she returned. Then, standing with her hands in front of her and perspiration shining on her forehead, she said, "You come wit' me."

Tamika gave a smile that would entice a snake out of a bird's nest. "You damn all *right*," she said.

Click-clack, click-clack, click-clack, click-clack, went Angela's little feet on the sidewalk. She and Ray were in front. Tamika and I trailed, and David was in between. Angela kept glancing back at him. We passed a doorway of a closed business where a grubby transient grabbed his crotch as we walked by.

155

Ahead, neon button lights chased around the office window of "The Bar None Motel." We passed through an arch and into the courtyard and came up on the short leg of an L where only one window glowed with light behind a shade. Angela went to that door and knocked one-two, one-two.

A small face, surrounded by dark hair, appeared as the door cracked open. It opened wider and the girl stepped back, her eyes darting from face to face.

Ray smoothly jostled Angela sideways as David and Tamika went in, then walked her a few steps back toward the street.

I followed the other two into the room. My cop training made me look in the bathroom. Behind the door on a hook was a white negligee. Over the shower rod a pair of white bikini panties were drying. A red silk rose lay on top of the medicine cabinet. And on the toilet tank was a slim plastic container holding salmon-colored condom packets. I picked one up and looked at it. Made in Japan.

Binky was sitting on the bed when I came back. She wore a gray nightshirt with Bugs Bunny in full-toothed grin on the front, and gray slippers with blue inner linings. The bed was turned back for only one person. The pillow was propped up as if she'd been watching TV before we came in, and indeed, the set was on, volume low, tuned to *Star Trek* on Channel 13. She backed up on the bed and tucked her legs under her.

David said, "We're here to help you." Her eyes shifted to him and held.

When Tamika spoke to her in Spanish, the girl shook her head vigorously, clearly alarmed.

"Interpret," I said.

"I asked if she is being kept here against her will."

I had taken one of the two chairs in the room, Ray stood,

and Tamika sat on the edge of the bed. Binky kept glancing at Ray with something I read as fear.

Tamika said something to her, fast, urgent. Then she turned to us and said, "She's coming with us. I told her that. She can stay at my place."

"What about Angela?" I said, concerned for her too.

Ray said, "We take one thing at a time."

Tamika got up and opened drawers in the small dresser in the corner. Binky stayed frozen in place. I found two plastic grocery bags in a drawer and handed one to Tamika, and as she stuffed things in them from other drawers, I went into the bathroom and got Binky's toothbrush and a small, flowered cosmetics bag. I glanced at the condoms—the same brand as those I found in the coffee packets in Turtle Rock—and took those too.

Then I went to the open closet-space opposite the bathroom and got a pair of sneakers, two folded tank-tops, and a clump of underpants off the shelf. A long red sweater was on a hanger. I pulled it off and brought it to Binky, who was now standing by the bed but cowed by Tamika's relentless energy as she slammed drawers, drew off a pillowcase, and filled it with clothes she couldn't fit in the plastic sack. David helped Binky put on the sweater. Then she got down and pulled from under the bed a pair of brown moccasins.

Now her expression was set to a timid determination. She crossed over to the other side of the bed and tipped up the lamp on the nightstand, retrieving a small sheaf of folded money, and thrust it into her sweater pocket. When she turned again to look at us, a shadow of a smile came over her face.

CHAPTER 23

Ray led the way. Tamika, with her plastic sacks in tow, walked beside Binky, and David and I brought up the rear. When we were almost to the archway, two men angled toward us from between the office and the first motel room.

Binky stopped, still as a bird sighting a cat, then stepped to the other side of Tamika while Ray slowed and his face grew hard.

The larger man called out, "Hey! *Pucha!*"

Binky whimpered.

"Hey, yourself, man," Ray said.

The larger man wore a dark leather jacket and a beige shirt, and had a tight, mean face. The smaller one had both his hands in his jacket pockets. I kept him in my sight, watching for cues.

Light from motel signs glowing on his leather jacket, the bigger one said to Ray, "Where you goin', Pancho?"

"No trouble, man," Ray said. "We're just going to our car."

"Fuck you are," lemon-face said. No one moved. I'd look back later and say it was a Mexican stand-off, but it didn't cross my mind at the time. "That one don't go with you," the guy said, thrusting his chin Binky's way.

David said, "Is your name Izzy?"

The man stared, then made a move past Ray and Tamika to reach for Binky. Ray jammed over and grabbed the guy's shirt in a fist, nearly lifting him off the ground, and shoved him away.

I pulled Binky back and stood in front of her. The little guy kept shifting weight, not sure of himself, keeping an eye on David. David moved closer to him. Then the big one came at Ray.

Ray blocked a punch, then his left flew out and slammed into the jerk's jaw so hard a string of spit laced over the dark air. The man landed quick and hard, unable to spare his head from the asphalt. It hit like a boot dropped on hardwood.

The little one had no impulse to join the fray. He backed up, palms forward while Ray was leaning over the first one, who was still down but trying to rise.

Ray dug into the gonzo's arm with plier-like fingers just above the elbow. The punk yelped so hard it rang around the court. "I don't have nothing, I don't have nothing, *fuck* you, man!"

Ray prepared to mash him again.

"Enough," I called to Ray. "Come on, let's go."

Tamika's Spanish vowels were tripping in that ripple-brook way, soft words, trying to placate.

Feeling for a weapon on the downed guy and coming up empty, Ray called him something in Spanish, then turned and approached the twerp David was covering. Ray shoved him and in an instant gained a control hold, then patted him and pulled a ditch-gun out of his sock. I got a sick knot in my stomach. It just as easily could have been drawn and used.

The little guy started chattering, "Okay, okay, okay. Lea' me 'lone, man. I done nothin' to you."

"Shut up," Ray said, and tucked the gun under his own shirt in back.

Lemon-Face rose on one elbow and whined, "Why you messin' with my gir'fren?"

"You mean her?" Ray said. "She your friend? You his friend?" Binky stood frozen. "I don't *think* so. Now get outta here. Go on!" Ray said, and moved like he was going to give the punk a kick. The punk scrambled up and hurried off with the other one. A few yards away, they both spat curses our way.

"Ask her who those guys were," Ray told Tamika. He was checking the car mirrors to see what might be coming up on us.

She did, and Binky paused ever so briefly, then said, "Julio." She looked down as if sorry to be giving up the name or sorry for a memory. "D'other one Izzy."

"Izzy! That's *him!* The coyote," David said. "I knew it!" He craned his head to look back, but we were too far away by now. In Binky's small face was the resigned dread of a kid watching for foot shadows to break the light under a bedroom door.

We sat like a family in Tamika's living room. Impressionist prints of women in pastels and parasols hung on the walls. Tamika, a woman of contrasts.

Ray was getting a big soda bottle to put on the coffee table, and a large bag of chips ripped down the middle, while Tamika brought glasses. Binky spoke with a sadness in her voice. I'd give the girl credit. Stressed or not, she tried to use English. "I know Izzy . . . *hijos*," Binky said.

"Since you were kids," Tamika said.

"*Si.* He go way. But . . . I see *mas*."

"Ask her his full name," I said.

Before she could, Binky answered, "Hector Corona Lizzaraga."

"Hector," I said.

She nodded. She told Tamika that Izzy was her brother Humberto's age. Hector was getting to be a big-shot in her village from his activities as a smuggler of persons. One time, Humberto decided to cross the border in the hope of sending money back to the family. Everything was so going well, until Humberto was killed by the *Norte Americanos* one night, in one of the gullies. "Bery bad mans," she said, tears welling in her eyes. From then on, Hector's price for getting people across went up. But Binky believed she should take her brother's place. For her mother, it had been the first time she could buy blankets for everyone.

David, sitting across from her, whispered, "Blankets."

She said, "Izzy . . . *loco*," her lips quivering. "My fren'," Binky said after a few moments, *"Fue asesinado."*

Tamika glanced at Ray.

Even I got that one. "Who was that, Binky?"

She wiped her nose on her red sweater, studied her lap for a moment, then said, "Her name Nita Estevez."

Ray hadn't known about Nita Estevez. It was a county case, nothing he'd be privy to. "A month ago," I said.

Binky nodded. Bunny teeth protruded in a fold between the sweater edges. Her face was heart-shaped, giving all the more effect to her helpless, childlike appearance.

"We're going to protect you, Binky. You know that, don't you?" I said. "Do you know who murdered your friend?"

"Izzy."

"Why would he do that?"

"Bery mad."

"What was he mad about, do you know?"

Softly, with a furtive glance toward Dave, she said, "He mad she no wanoo fock guys."

It was after two when I got home. Tomorrow I'd call the guys at Homicide and deal with whatever criticism was due. For now I was too exhausted to think.

I had three messages on my answering machine. I pressed the button and let them play. The first was from Mary Langston. She wondered if her grandson could come see the guinea pig. The second was from Joe: "Checkin' in, kiddo. Call me in the morning. I may get turned loose tomorrow. Love ya." Joe, using the L word, which we don't do . . . so much commitment. Joe, coming home!

My thoughts flipped to David, sleeping on Ray's couch now. Knowing I could hear the next message from the machine, I drifted in to the laundry room to check on Motorboat. His blond head was sticking out of the log, nose working hard against the shadows: That you?

I bent over the cage and lifted the lid. His pod-seed eyes were as intense as a mad man's. "It's me, little guy. Just me." I pinched some alfalfa out of the nearby sack and lowered the stiff stems in. Ever-Ready beastie snatched the stalks, which jerked now in motion like a nervous green mustache.

The voice on the third message took me a moment to place: Gil. For a moment I felt disoriented, even intruded upon. "Thought I'd just say hi," he said. "Been thinking of you a lot. Wanted to ask if you'd like to go out to Hemet this weekend, see a train museum."

I walked back into the kitchen to hear the rest.

" 'Course I don't know if that sort of thing would interest you at all. But give a call. We could take in Palm Springs, *great* about now. And hey, you know what? Some group is moving the heron nests. Too much doo-doo and fish heads raining down. Moving them with a crane and a truck. Audubon's trying to make them wait till the hatchlings are grown, but in case the city wonks do anything funny, a bunch of us are going down to stage a protest under the pines. Want to join us, be a heron hero? Now if that doesn't get your interest, what would?"

Gil finished with, "Really, Smokey, I'd use just about any excuse to see you again. Call me?" Pushy, this guy. But I smiled. I could be a heron hero, but I could also be a fool. Not now. But sometime. Gil. Joe. Don't think about it.

I fell into bed and awoke an hour later, seeing Nita Estevez with her battered body; smelling the smell; hearing Binky whimper, and the Doe on the hill raising his head and spilling blood from his mouth as he stared at me.

I got up and drank water and gazed at the darkened bay, then went back and forced myself to see flowers blazing along the bluffs where a developer generously spread seed before he mangled the tract with two-story boxes covered in Spanish tile.

CHAPTER 24

I walked into Stu's office and pulled a chair directly in front of his desk. "Stu, you can fire me, you can fire me two weeks from now, but I have to tell you something you're not going to like. And I have to ask you for something at the same time."

He looked up over new granny glasses and put his pencil down. "Let's have it," he said, and not irritably.

I handed him a chart I made before leaving the house:

Doe 1:	Technology Park	Desi Cono Blanco ("Whitey")	KNEW #4?
Doe 2:	Nellie Gail	Still un-ID'd	
Doe 3:	Turtle Rock	Froylan Marcos Cordillo (Freddie")—Joyride	KNEW #1? DAVID KNEW NITA E. KNEW
Doe 4:	San Juan Creek	Victor Minor Montalvo	DAVID KNEW
Nita Estevez:	Dresden St.	Joyride w/ Freddie	BINKY KNEW
"Izzy"	G. Cheng's asso.	Suspect for Estevez? Turtle Rock?	BINKY KNOWS
Greg Cheng:	D's roommate	Knows Izzy, Freddie. Who else?	DAVID KNOWS

It took him a while to absorb. He asked a fair number of questions. "Please, Stu, this can't get back to Joe."

"We'll see," he said.

I was breaking a boy's trust and feared for his father as well, but I said, "I'll trust you to know the right time."

Stu sat back and put both hands on the arms of his chair. "Smokey, I don't know if you know I am married to a woman of Mexican heritage."

"No, Stu, I didn't know that." Just pick me up off the floor.

"I'm not going to waste time chewing on you, even though you deserve it. What I want you to do is get in touch with the investigators on these cases without delay."

"I will. I know it's time. But can you understand—"

"About Joe?" He brushed his bald head and said, "Do you think this happened from teaching kindergarten?"

"Thanks, Stu."

"Now, what about this boy of Sanders's? Has he ever been in trouble with the law?"

"Never . . . er, that we know of." Stu looked at me skeptically. "I mean, I guess nothing surprises me any more."

"Where is he now?"

"In the keeping of a CHP officer friend of ours."

"Well, I hope he'll whack some sense in him. Now get to work, Brandon. You think this is a social club?"

"Thanks, Stu. Thank you very much for understanding," I said, getting up and sliding back the chair.

"I didn't say you were off the hook. We'll talk later."

"Right," I said, and turned to leave, and looked back and said thanks again.

Joe wasn't getting out today. "I blipped when I should have blapped," he said. "They want to keep me a while longer." He sounded depressed. He also asked if I'd seen David at all. I told him I thought David was spending some time with Ray Vega. "They hit it off, huh? Terrific."

"You mind the medics now. I'll come see you soon as I can."

"Latuh, gatuh," he said.

I met Boyd Russell for lunch at a sandwich shop downtown. He said, "What's this about?" as we were walking to get in line.

"I know someone who knew the Capistrano Doe. Not well, but knew him. This person was also acquainted with the Doe found in Turtle Rock, Will's case."

"Yah?" he said, then studied the menu board over the heads of three other customers in line. "Who is it?" He was wearing a yellow shirt with his brown suit. In the angle of the sunlight, the channels in his chin and lip looked like beard growth.

"There's more," I said, and waited till we got our sandwiches and sat outside. I felt relief, yet a certain dread.

Boyd took out a pen and notepad after we sat down. "Who is this guy? I'll give a call."

"Well, Boyd, there's a little problem there." He looked at me, pen poised. "You know Joe Sanders."

He nodded, giving me a funny look. "Of course."

"Right. Well. . . ."

"How's he doing?"

"Not perfect. I'm worried, matter of fact. He was supposed to be released today. Then something kept them from it."

"So Joe's the one knows these dead taco-burners?" He laughed to acknowledge the idea was absurd.

"Not exactly," I said. "It may be, though, his son does."

Boyd took a copy of the chart I compiled and promised to keep it to himself for the time being. He'd run checks on

Hector Lizzaraga and Binky Jalindo. He said I should, however, be prepared to have him and Bright interview David
shortly. I was grateful to him for the breathing room.
Somehow I didn't expect it from him. "This Binky," he said,
"we'll want to talk to her too."

When he was done with his lunch, he leaned back in his
chair and yawned. He pulled out a pack of Camels, tapped
one out, and said, "Not much sleep last night." Then he
looked at me and asked, "You ever been married?"

At the end of the day I ran into Harold Raimey. "Give that
old geezer Joe Sanders a message for me, okay? I'd call him
myself, but my wife's waiting on me, we're going up to Ar-
rowhead."

"Sure, Harold."

"Tell him we got hold of Charles Dobson's exercise shoes.
Got a good match to the plaster cast y'all made. It's not
enough yet to send invitations to the hangin', but we'll get
there."

"I know you will," I said.

"Give 'im a kiss for me, too," he said, waving as he walked
off.

I dialed Joe's number just before leaving and got no answer.

On the way home I stopped to get gas and bought three
lottery tickets even though the big pot had been won the night
before: 20 million to a leaf raker who says he'll keep working
just because he loves his job.

At home I tried Joe again. No answer. I rang up the recep-
tion desk. It took a while for the woman to look up the room
record. Joe had been moved again. "Where to?" I asked.

"I'm afraid he's gone back to IC."

I was at Hoag Hospital in twenty minutes. I'd blown

through the yellows at intersections and was angry at the slow pedestrians making their way on the crosswalk to the hospital front door.

I got blocked at the nurse's station by ICU. The nurse asked who I was looking for. When I told her, she said, "Not just now. Why don't you call in the morning?"

"I will call in the morning. But I'm here now."

"I just gave him his meds. He's about gone," she said, then realized how dire that sounded. "Asleep," she said.

"If you just gave him meds, he must still be awake."

We stared at each other, a war of emotion over profession.

"Are you a relative, Miss . . . ?"

"Look, it's only a little after seven."

"I have seven-thirty-five."

"He never goes to sleep this early."

"Are you his daughter?"

"A friend."

"Why don't you talk with the doctor tomorrow?" she said. "I think that'd be a better idea."

I could tell her the better idea I had. But didn't.

CHAPTER 25

Ray was home, off-watch/on-call. He said, "We lost Binky. She slipped David when he went to his old apartment to get clothes."

"Damn! Where's David?"

"He's here. You want to talk to him?"

"I guess. Jeez."

"He's in the john. When he comes out."

I told Ray I finally went to Homicide with the info and they were going to work with us. "Wise girl, kid."

"Except they want to talk to Binky."

"Tough titty. She's vam-ooso."

"Well, I'm sorry for her, but you know what, Ray? Maybe it's best. For David, I mean. I hope she makes it though. Where would a girl like that go, out there in the world, no English?"

"She'll get along, believe me."

"I hope you're right, Raymond."

He put David on.

"I have *so* messed up," he said. "But I'm going to find her. I think what happened is Greg or that creep Izzy saw her sitting in my car. I worried about leaving her there, but I worried more about bringing her in. It was so stupid."

"David, I have something to tell you. Your father's back in Intensive Care. They wouldn't even let me see him tonight."

"Oh, Christ."

"I think you'd better call your mother."

"I will."

Noreen Ayres

I could hear the sadness in his voice but I had to go on. "David, I have something else to tell you. I have broken my promise to you."

"No! What if it gets back to Dad now?"

"If it works the way I think, we may be able keep it from him indefinitely. That is, if you have truly told us everything. Have you, David?"

"Yes!"

"Good, then." I told him he needed to pick a time when he could come in and talk to Boyd Russell.

"And what about Binky? What about *her*?"

"Dave, please. Will you wait for my call in the morning, after I set up a time with Boyd Russell? Let's do it in an orderly way."

"When will you call me?"

"Figure about eight. I need time to be sure to reach him."

"All right," he said, but I knew that could change with the wind.

I talked to Ray again, said I needed to catch some sleep. "Hey, keep an eye on our boy, huh?"

"I'm doin' what I can. But I can't put an ankle monitor on him, you know."

"I do know, Ray. Thanks, old bud."

"Here to serve," he said. Then he said, "Tamika's here. She wants to say something to you."

She came on and said, about Binky, "She's just a baby, barely seventeen. That evil prick's got her paying off what she don't need to. If you guys catch that puke, hold him so I can take a turn."

I smiled. "Can you remember anything Binky said that might indicate where she would go?"

"I think she'll go back to the motel."

"Why would she go back there?"

170

"Moths go to flame. I've seen it a lot. That girl, that Nita she was talking about? She thinks Lizard did it. He told Binky once, you don't behave, you wind up like her."

"Yet you think. . . ."

"Like I said. Listen, there's a word she used belongs to somebody older than her. *Aguantar.* It means to put up with things you can't change."

That night I slept—overslept. As soon as I could muster, I phoned Hoag to find out how Joe was doing. Same. Then I raced to work and phoned Homicide soon as I could. Boyd said he could see David late afternoon, maybe four. Perfect.

I went into Stu's and told him what had evolved, that I'd be taking off early to bring David to Boyd Russell. "I don't need a report every half-hour, Brandon," he said. "End results is what I'm interested in." He was standing at a file cabinet, fingers stuck in a folder, glasses down on his nose. I smiled and thanked him.

I returned to my desk and dialed Ray's house. "You're there."

"Not long for these parts, though. I'm outta here."

"How's the kid?"

"I'm lookin' at him right now, hunkered over a plate of scrambled eggs and Tabasco."

"He's set up to talk to someone at four," I said.

"I might have to tranq him before I leave. He thinks he's ten feet tall and bullet-proof. Wants to go find Binky or confront that guy Cheng."

"Oh no-no-no. Put him on, will you?"

I sweated it during the day, wondering if he'd show. I really didn't need a complication with Boyd if David did a rabbit on me.

171

Somewhere in the hours that clipped by I got a chance to call Joe again. A nurse gave him a phone, because he wasn't allowed out of bed. Our conversation seemed . . . I don't know . . . strained. Maybe he was plain exhausted from it all. I was guarded, I suppose for David's sake, and my own. He did say, "I'm sure putting my friends on a rough track, eh?"

"Oh, Joe. . . ."

"Ah, it's all right. Probably just too much lime Jell-O."

"That could be so."

"You doin' good?"

"Muddling along. Slow on the Doe cases." Then, "What I want to know is how, you, Superman, can break a case while sitting on your ass, eating lime Jell-O? I saw Harold Raimey."

"Yeah?"

"Don't get over-excited."

"Tell me."

"He got Charles Dobson's tennis shoes. Your cast shots help a bunch. He's re-visiting the alibi, and there's an insurance policy and a mother-in-law who says Mrs. Dobson was seeking divorce."

"Far out!" Joe said.

David showed as promised. We met Boyd at a Red Robin restaurant in Tustin. The two men shook hands, then David and I slid into the red naugahyde booth opposite.

In the next hour, Boyd Russell showed just how good an interviewer he could be. He surprised me. Probing and casually making light jokes by turns, he soon put David at ease. When the kid got some potato skins stuffed with bacon and cheese in him, it was like he'd known the rumpled cop a long time.

The only place Dave stumbled was when Binky's name came up. He was still stricken by his own actions and worried that she may be in harm's way. At the last mention of her name, David gave me a quick glance, wrung his hands under the table, and said, "I have more to tell you. You know I knew Freddie, the one killed at Turtle Rock."

"Yes, right. And. . . ."

"And I recognized that one you found down in Capistrano."

"My case," Boyd said, looking at me, then David.

David took a moment to gather himself. He looked away, then told us, "Binky's friend, Nita? She was in love with a guy named Carlos. Carlos Sarmiento."

Boyd was writing this on his little notepad.

David waited till he looked up, then said, "He's dead too."

Boyd cut his eyes at me and waited.

David was talking to me now. "I was so afraid. Afraid it would get to my folks, this whole mess. I had been with Binky by that time."

"I understand."

"Well, you know that Juan Doe that was found in Nellie Gail Ranch?" His words were crackling in the hollow of his mouth. He paused and took a drink.

Indeed I do, I thought. We had nothing for that one yet.

Boyd's face said it all. This was it. The kid across the table from him was going to crack our cases for us. Maybe. The whole noisy room seemed to float in a gelatin of soundlessness, no noise anywhere, as we waited for David to go on.

"I told you I'd only seen Binky a couple of times. In reality, I must have gone up there four, five times. A week or so after Nita died," he said, "Angela told me Nita's boyfriend got whacked too. She asked if I could get a gun."

"Angela asked *you?*" I said.

"She was scared. I asked her of who. Izzy, she said. That's when I really started getting worried for Binky. I didn't know what to do. And that's why," David said, "when I talked to you at the Swallow's Parade that day, I was just trying to sort things out."

Boyd said, "Did you get that girl a gun?"

"No! I wouldn't touch a gun."

"Good," Boyd said, the frown relaxing some. "So," he said, "this guy Whitey's real name is Carlos Sarmiento?" Boyd was looking down now at his notepad.

"Wrong. Whitey's name was Desi Blanco."

"Desi Cono Blanco," I said. "Technology Park."

Boyd acknowledged but was clearly confused.

David said, "So put it together: Nita first. Then her boyfriend, Carlos. Or, no . . . maybe it was Whitey first. Anyway, Greg Cheng is *central* to this, I'm telling you. You wonder why I'm sleeping in the bushes? Now you understand?" He looked around at the crowd as if he could find someone threatening there.

I said, touching David's arm, "I see what you've been going through."

"And there's Dad," he said hoarsely.

"And there's Dad," I said.

CHAPTER 26

I walked to David's car with him. "How do you feel about Boyd Russell?" I asked.

"I guess I'm glad I talked to him."

"Do you trust him?"

"I think so."

"What are you going to do now? Want to come to my place? We could call the hospital, see how your dad's doing."

"Not tonight, thanks. I'm pretty wiped."

"I imagine."

"About Binky?" His eyes showed feeling. "She has great spirit. I know a teeny bit of Spanish. *'Espiritu.'* "

"I like the sound of it," I said.

"Yeah," he answered, fingers tucked in his front pockets. *"Espiritu."* He bent and gave me a quick hug. Then I watched him weave between cars until he reached his.

Joe still couldn't have visitors. I'd have to find someone to make me some false ID so I could get in as a relative; there was plenty around.

I'd been home an hour when Gil Vanderman called. I told him sorry, no Hemet, no train museum this weekend.

"Can I see you tonight, cup of coffee at least?"

"It's been a long day."

"Well, I can understand that. I haven't always gotten to work at doing what I love. I used to be a computer pro- grammer. Don't ever work for a computer company. They'll work you into the ground. Now that I've told you my sordid past, does it kill any possible interest you might have been developing for me?" He had a nice voice, a sense of humor.

"Gil, it's like this a lot with me. And I *am* seeing someone."

"You told me that. I'm just calling as a friend."

"Maybe you better find another friend, Gil. I don't mean that to sound harsh, it's just. . . ."

"Hey, you have a great weekend, hear?"

"I will. You too."

I wanted to go somewhere. Where, I didn't know. Just go. So I drove to Triangle Square, a shopping center in Newport with gobs of neon and live music coming from the second-story deck. I went into the music store to look for Mungo Jerry on a CD because I'd seen a finch on my balcony, his red-orange cap like a tiny yarmulke, and he piped a series of notes that sounded like two bars of "In the Summertime": When the weather's hot, he's got women, he's got women on his mind. At the section for Hits of the Seventies and Eighties, I felt a presence close to me and stepped aside, still reading labels.

"Don't run. I just got here," Gil said.

"What are *you* doing here?"

"They didn't throw the lock soon enough, I guess."

He had on a peach-colored shirt with a duck embroidered on the pocket. He was looking for music too, jazz. He didn't press me, didn't recriminate, and soon wandered on to find his selection. At the cash register he glanced at me twice, and I, of course, at him, or I wouldn't have known. He came back.

We had our coffee out on the veranda where the guitar player was performing. He told me about a place called Sid's just a block or two away, a little dive with a banana tree by the door, good music inside. Come check it out. Leave any time you want.

I drove over, following him. We listened to a small blues band, the two of us and six other people, and sat on hard wooden chairs at a table covered in vinyl cloth; just about as unglamorous as it could be. In the brown shadows, Gil leaned over and kissed me by the side of the mouth. The band started in on livelier music. I was momentarily happy, cut free of the outer world.

When we left an hour later, outside Gil kissed me again: under the hard light in the parking lot. Through my car window, rolled down. "Come home with me," he whispered, still leaning in. He put his warm lips on the flesh next to my ear.

"I can't."

"Come home with me."

"On your way, cad."

"Walk with me, just a little bit."

"I have to get home."

"The air's so warm. The night's so beautiful." He unlocked my door, reaching inside. "Walk with me. Then I'll let you go home. I promise. Look at that moon."

And why . . . and why shouldn't sex be like saying hello? I know how most people view such things. I know that to preserve the peace, the social order, such private notions should be kept private. I know that for most people anything beyond one-at-a-time moments of the heart is unthinkable. Shall I say then, merely, that somewhere in the ticking night I heard a dove release its yearning sound. We give comfort, get comfort, where we can.

Later I stood at my kitchen window and watched the sky grow silver in that moment when the world holds its breath between dark and light. I told myself I would phone Joe first thing, get grounded again. Joe, alone and bored and scared and angry at the fate that was his, and no doubt still asleep at this hour.

I saw the silhouettes of homes on the far bluffs and thought of the lives therein, more coming into the county every day: 3000 new streets added to county maps this year alone. I thought of the people who were up already: weary mothers with sick babies, cops on graveyard, *indocumentados* making their way to pick-up points where drivers would invite them to work construction sites or kitchens, or the gardens of rich people's homes. I thought of Binky and of Nita Estevez, and of Trudy Kunitz grappling with her ordeal.

In the quiet reeds beyond, the sun would soon begin to penetrate. Life would stir in the waters, creatures would search, feed, and mate. *And it is good,* saieth the prophet. Why, then, this restless sadness? And why, then, did I wish I could erase the night and begin again? I had only said hello.

CHAPTER 27

Saturday morning David called and said he was going back to his apartment to get his things. If Cheng was there, he was there. He'd handle it. He could also tell Cheng that Binky was hands-off, wherever she was.

What a mess of nerves and random behavior.

I tried talking him out of it and asked where Ray was. Ray had left for work. But there had to be discomfort in David's own plan or he wouldn't have called *me*. I said, "I'm coming along."

When we got there we took a path to a wooden fence at the rear, where David reached over and opened the gate. On the patio were plants blooming in a dozen pots. David said, "Greg's."

He unlocked a door that led to the kitchen. Except for a soda can on the counter and a newspaper separated on the table, the place looked spotless. The living room had a ruby-colored Oriental rug and a handsome red leather couch, not the version you might normally see in a student's abode, but the expensive kind whose seams were tapped with brass tacks around its curves. Paisley drapes hung at the windows. A small table held a chess game.

"Greg's here," David said.

I saw the reflection of a computer screen in one of the windows, coming off a room to the left. Then Greg Cheng came out.

He was a little more than my height but stocky, and wore pants that bagged at the hem over puffy feet, and a green plaid shirt over a white crew-neck. A chunk of his hair fell to his eyebrow like an arrow pointing to the round, soft features of his face. "You," he said to David. "I thought you decided you couldn't live here any more."

"I have stuff to get," David said.

Cheng swept a hand toward the hallway. "Be my guest." He had an ever-present grin, as if it were all a joke. Cheng looked at me. "Welcome to my humble jumble."

"I want to talk first," David said, and nodded to a chair.

"M-m-m, I'm a little busy right now. But Dave, I know you'll pay what's owed on rent and utilities when the time comes."

"You're a piece of dog shit, Cheng. And I'm going to dig a hole and bury you." He said this leaning in, as if ready to spring.

I stepped forward to calm him.

Cheng looked from him to me, then said, "Nice meeting you, then. Excuse me," and eased back into the room from whence he came, shutting the door.

"The prick," David said under his breath, then went to the room that was his and pulled a zippered suitcase from a closet. He threw in the few remaining clothes he had, and books from a dresser top, then moved a table to jerk cords out of the wall that led to a small radio and CD player. He stuffed the unit and a pile of CD's into the bag along with some other odds and ends from the bathroom, then looked around the room and said, "I don't care about the rest of this stuff."

In the hallway, David set his bag down and made a move toward Greg's door just as it opened.

"Are we done?" Greg asked.

The guy did have a smack-inspiring style about him.

David's jaw muscles were working. "It's all I can do not to bust you in the chops, Greg, so don't make it worse. Now you

180

listen to me: I want you and that asshole Lizzaraga to keep away from Binky, completely away." He was trying to be a man, where he'd failed before.

"I have very little interest in what Hector Lizzaraga does with his placements, other than those which I require for assistance in my business activities. But I'll tell you what. If I see that young lady around anywhere, I will certainly give her wide berth."

"You do that, you pond scum."

Cheng actually chuckled at that. Then he said, "As far as Izzy goes, it may be she has already made her choice: him over you."

David lunged forward. I yelled his name, then saw he'd only ripped Greg's beeper off him. It was clenched in his hand. "You get in touch with that asshole before I get to Binky and I'll see to it you are hurt in a way that can't be fixed. Got it, butt-face?"

Cheng looked pale. I said, "Come on, Dave, it's time to go."

His eyes stayed fixed on his former roommate as we headed to the door. In the car again, he said, "I think I know where she might be."

CHAPTER 28

A hidden lake, he said. Not on any maps. "I looked. There's no blue patch off El Toro Road. It's where they bring some of the new ones. A migrant crash-pad until they find work."

"This would be Binky who told you this."

"Angela. I went up there last night."

"You *what?*"

"Ray was in bed. I told him I was going out for ice cream. He was asleep when I got back. I can't help it," he said. "I feel responsible."

"You're not."

"Why are *you* here with me if you don't care?"

"I guess my coat's caught in the car door, hon."

"Same thing," he said with a sad grin.

I persuaded David to let Ray in on what he wanted to do. Ray fussed, then said wait a while. He'd be off at five and come help.

In the intervening hours we called Joe. Doctors were with him now, a nurse said. We couldn't talk, but I was appeased to hear he was much improved, arguing with them and cracking wise.

When Ray showed up he said to David, "So, you're on the trail, huh, buddy?"

Dave looked a little sheepish. "It's a start."

Ray was wearing tan pants and a Hawaiian shirt with big white flowers on a green background. I made a crack about it and he said "I wish I'd been born rich instead of so good-lookin'." Then he said to David, "You figure Binky's out there at this lake place."

"That's what Angela says. I don't know why she'd go back there, but. . . ."

"We've checked three maps," I said. "Let's just take a drive."

"You got it," Ray said. "Why don't you bring that piece of Tupperware you got?" I asked where his service piece was. "I mean for extra. You just never know."

I went to a small safe in my closet and got out my Glock, made mostly of plastic but deadly all the same. I put on loose pants with large pockets, set my pocket holster inside and the Glock in it, and was ready to ride.

Once outside, David said to wait a minute, and he went to his car and brought out Binky's red sweater. He didn't say why, and Ray and I glanced at each other but didn't say anything either. The heart has reasons, for a 20-year-old boy. . . .

When Dave climbed in, Ray said, "Ready, sport?"

We drove El Toro twice before finally pulling over to reconnoiter. That it was growing dark didn't help. The road passes through a congested channel of strip malls until it gives into open country with rolling hills and old oak like a step into real country.

On the third pass, we crept along so slowly cars blew horns at us. But then we saw a narrow dirt road. Thirty yards in was a flimsy wire gate. Dave got out and opened it. We drove through, and then he got back in, a growing alertness on his face. The road went on for a while, and then we passed giant wood-framed tubs holding dead starter trees, and I realized this was an abandoned nursery. Nursery was big business in the county, but this one hadn't made it. Ray drove slowly, gauging the land. Ahead, a covered porch came into view at the end of a tunnel of six eucalyptus trees; then the roof, and the side of the building.

We parked and got out. On a limb of chaparral a hawk hunkered like an old man full of grudges. A gust of wind blew through the trees and made the eucalyptus branches sway, and brought to our hearing something like a chime, as of ice being stirred in a glass.

Ray walked ahead, the flowers of his shirt falsely bright in the dimness around us. He mounted the porch and peered into the low windows of the house while Dave and I stood off. Ray tried the door, went in, then stepped out of the cabin and said, "All clear."

There were three rooms divided by flimsy imitation-wood partitions. The first showed only food wrappers and indentations in the low-grade carpet where desks or chairs had once sat.

The second had a ratty twin mattress on the floor covered with a dark blue blanket. Next to it was a six-pack of creme soda still linked in its plastic hood, and a package of Oreo cookies. A magazine called *Shooter's World* lay on the floor. That room had the only rear window to let in light.

In the last room was a twin bed with a "pencil" headboard, its narrow wood slats spaced an inch apart. Sections of white nylon rope streamed down from each of the four posts. On the bare mattress was a flat, stained pillow, no case.

"Wonderful," I said.

I felt Dave behind me. In a low voice he said, "Surely she wasn't here?" His face showed anguish.

Ray, behind us, said, "Somebody was. Recently." He nodded back to where the unopened creme soda was.

An old, overstuffed chair blocked the foot of the bed. Nestled in the angle between the arm and back was an empty cigarette pack with the Harley-Davidson logo, and a bean can with dead matches and stubs in the bottom. The chair wasn't all the way back against the wall. I looked behind. Used condoms lay in an ugly mass.

"See anything?" Ray asked.

"No," I said, pulling back off the chair. I'd spare David that.

Outside on the porch we could see a half-moon shying from incoming clouds above the tops of distant trees. I wished for a cleansing hurricane where none was bound to come.

We headed down a path toward the lake. The body of water was small, maybe the size of two basketball courts. Brush rose at different levels, some three times our height, and the scent of sage, creosote, eucalyptus, decay, and toxic lake filled the air.

Two tiny eyes broke the water's surface as the path curved to the bank. A knot of gnats hurled our way, whirled around our heads, then departed as quickly as it came.

Such silence here, yet the city bare miles away.

David said, "It's a fool's errand." He meant, of course, the girl with the small face and melted brown-sugar eyes was not here. I hoped she never had been. Some people think that what Tamika does for a living and what I did at one time myself is one rung away from sewer-flow. But there is low and there is lower.

We saw headlights on a high ridge and the outline of a truck against the faint horizon. Ray said, "Stake-bed, occupied five times, two in front. Worker-bees coming home to roost."

"Not this road," I said. "That's another one."

I looked toward the entrance where we came in and saw nothing. An American coot shot across the lake on tiptoes, leaving a milky wake. The North Star was livening. I saw a hawk slide down an invisible string to the earth.

We heard the tinkling sound again. "It's close," Ray said, narrowing his eyes.

I said, "What would you think of getting a dog out here?"

Ray studied me, while David's face showed hope. "Why bring out the posse?" Ray said. "We don't even know what we have here, if anything."

"The department wouldn't be involved. Believe it or not, I know a handler, a civilian, lives right down the road here, on a street called Hunky Dory Lane."

"Hunky Dory Lane."

"It's true. It's on the map, I didn't make it up. Her name is Rosellen Richards. We met four years ago on a hike in the Saddlebacks."

David said, "You think she'd come?"

"One way to find out," Ray said, and gave me a wink. Humor him, it said. "We even have scenting material, right, bud? That red sweater."

A look of great satisfaction that maybe he'd done something right flooded over the boy's face, as he looked back toward the shack with the debris inside and out.

We trounced back through the brush and grasses. Ahead, a rabbit hopped across the path, halted, became a rock with ears, then bounded off.

Ray retrieved his cell phone from a pocket in the door of his truck, and I dialed Rosellen and I gave her the rundown. She came back with an unqualified, "Sure!"

My two *compadres* stood leaning against the raised porch, ankles crossed like cowhands talking over where to put the next post-hole. I felt curiously heartened, maybe just from the illusion that we were *doing* something. I remembered Rosellen telling me once, "Bloods fall dead last on the intelligence scale out of 140 breeds," she told me, "but if you can tolerate bad hips, poor eyesight, loud snores, a tendency toward cancer, and fountains of slobber, you'll have a sweet companion."

Now she asked, "You want a trail dog or a cadaver dog?"

"Not a body dog. As far as we know it's not a crime scene, and if it were I wouldn't want to compromise it."

"That's too bad," she said, "because she's only trained with pig parts, and I'd sure like to try her on human."

We returned in the truck to the entrance to wait for her. At one point David said, "You think Binky's dead, don't you?"

Ray reached across me and clapped David on the leg. "After this, we ride up to Santa Ana again. Deal?"

"Deal," the boy said.

Rosellen's headlights came easing around the big bend on El Toro. When we got her through the gate and Ray was driving back to the site, he said, "Hmp, she's pretty." And she is. Brown hair, good facial construct, and a body shown to advantage in jeans.

At the building, she slid open the door of her van, opened the cage, and brought her hound named Madam. The dog was already drooling great strands of slobber and shivering from excitement. Madam wore a metal-studded Martingale harness that went around her shoulders and between the forelegs to form a Y on the chest. She was alternately pulling on her leash, dancing, and peeing in the road.

"I keep her on six feet of lead and never work without a lantern," Rosellen said when I warned her of the possibility of hidden barbed wire. She showed us the flashlight on her forearm and clicked it on with a finger.

David gave her Binky's sweater. She bunched it under Madam's nose. *"Geo-Say,"* she commanded in Navajo, and

Madam took off in a steady tug, the rest of us plowing behind.

She went straight up the porch and into the building, her brindle tail twirling like a pinwheel. When she reached the back room, the dog barked once and once only, but joy shone in her eyes as she looked at her owner.

Rosellen praised her and said, "She found her scent right off. There's been cases where a dog was so morose from not finding someone she would grieve for days and maybe die. Yes, yes, so they say. Where else now, you want to look?"

We went outside again, and Rosellen gave the "hunt 'em up" command. Madam's nose was down and her tail twirling as she led us through the bushes in what seemed an aimless way. Willow, mulefat, and castor bean whipped us as we filed through.

Hearing the gentle jinging, Rosellen pulled up and said, *"Kee ki wah,"* then sent her light high across the brush. Ray's small mag light traced it too. Something gleamed in the chaparral.

"What the hell? Look at this," Ray said. We came closer and saw dangling from a tree limb a windchime made of printed-circuit boards bound with copper wire. The chromed edges hit together; the plastic layers gave only a soft tapping.

"Somebody's cute trail marker," Rosellen said.

Madam pulled us onward. She broke into a lope and Rosellen had to call her down a bit. The dog went a few more yards pulling hard, then stopped, was absolutely silent, dropped her hindquarters and urinated.

"Big-time find," Rosellen whispered.

With a fair moon now overhead, Ray said, "Let's shut the lights." Another gentle gust of wind and a tinkling of PCB chimes, stereophonic now.

We eased around a broad stand of pampas towering fifteen feet high, and made out an entryway built into the side of a cut-away hill. The front was shielded with a door made of close-set cane—*arundo donax,* to be exact. Rosellen dropped a hand to Madam's back. The animal shivered from one end to the other.

Then a stubby hand slid the cane door back, and a voice sounded from within.

"Welcome to my humble jumble," Cheng said.

CHAPTER 29

Cheng held a pistol. A .40 or .45. He was a lefty.

"Greg!" David cried hoarsely.

Rosellen commanded, *"Ko Coween, Ko Coween,"* meant to quiet her growling dog whose rigid form seemed ready to burst from its platform of earth.

Cheng's gaze took in Ray. This one was the threat. This one.

I moved tighter up to Ray so I could hide my hand as I slipped it into my pocket. Cheng said, "We meet again. You are trespassing on private property. You must leave."

Binky came forward from the shadows behind Greg, her eyes large, luminous, and void. She had the Bugs Bunny shirt on.

David cried out her name. Madam barked, her tail flicking madly, her rear portion carried side-to-side with the force of the movement. Rosellen stilled her and slowly moved backward. Yanking Binky under his arm, Greg held her there and told us again to leave.

Ray flicked on his flashlight, Binky tugged away from Cheng's hold, and Cheng divided his attention.

That's all that was needed. Ray was in motion, leaping forward, striking out for the weapon. The flashlight plopped into the brush and stared like a wild eye.

In the next few moments there was yelling, grunting, growling, and barking, and what I knew for sure was that Binky had fled into David's arms by nearly running over me, Rosellen was shouting *"Ko Coween!"* to Madam yards away, and I stood jostling for a good mark with my gun pointed ahead. What was behind Cheng, in the cave? Know your target, know your target: That was my training and I couldn't let go.

Cheng collapsed onto the ground, knocking the raft of cane down on top of them. The pistol exploded, the sound deafening, even outdoors.

My heart leapt. Where was Ray? I plunged forward, heaved the cane door off them with my left arm and shoulder, and aimed my weapon at Cheng's temple. "Give it up, give it up!" I screamed.

Then Ray was on him, jerking Cheng's pistol away. He put a knee on Cheng's arm, while Cheng screamed in pain and dug fingers into the earth.

Ray dropped the gun's magazine, ejected the round in the chamber, then tossed the weapon aside. He smacked Cheng with an open hand, then a backhand in quick succession, and yelled, "Pull down on me, will ya, you worthless piece o' shit!"

He rolled Cheng over, feeling for other weapons. Cheng made the mistake of moving. Ray smacked him again and ended his search with a heavy kick to Cheng's buttocks.

It made me wince, but what the public doesn't know nor would want to accept is that kicking a subject is an allowable increment in "level-of-force" technique. Wiggle a finger, breathe too hard, you get clobbered. I said, "We got him, Ray. He's done."

Ray pulled back. "Stay there and don't move, you little shit."

Cheng stayed still as a stump. Ray grabbed up his flashlight and shone it in the hutch while we both still covered Cheng. Inside were several storage boxes and flats of soda cans.

"I own this property! You're trespassing! I'll have you arrested."

"Arrest *this,* you slimey piece o' puke," Ray said, and kicked him again, this time in the thigh. Cheng yelped.

Then gunfire with a hot-yellow flash tore through the darkness. I threw myself to the ground and rolled. Ray jumped inside the cave, then darted out again, crouching. Greg Cheng was gone, and branches were switching.

Another blast flared, but I knew it wasn't from Cheng: not the sound of a .45; something lighter. A second shot, and I heard the round pass through the bushes. I flattened to the ground and let out a grunt of relief when I realized I wasn't the only one who couldn't shoot for shit.

"You all right?" Ray said from his spot.

"Yes," I whispered.

Over by the cabin a terrible howling lanced the night: Madam, having her say. I silently begged that Rosellen, David, and Binky were safe. A second howl set hairs on end. Ray made his way to my side. "Two o'clock," he said. I nodded. The shooter at two, with us the center of target.

"It's not Cheng. Who the hell is it?"

We eased away, cutting a crescent in the direction that would bring us behind the shooter. Ray stopped, touched my collarbone with a finger and pointed back toward the cabin. He'd keep going, take a ridge that ran parallel but more in line with the shooter.

"Keep your head down," he whispered.

Beyond the ridge, a car ignition ground and caught and a radio came on, a guy singing how he was a ramblin' man. Just as suddenly, it cut off. There was another way in, then, maybe an offshoot of the road the stake-bed truck used. That was why Cheng was here yet we saw no other cars. "He's leaving," I said.

"Don't count on it," Ray said. Then his finger went to his lips to shush me. I heard it too: a woman's voice, thin and plaintive. Then the sound of splashing. Again Ray pointed back toward the building. I'd go after the splash, counter-clockwise. "Can you handle it?"

"No problem," I said, and believed it, whatever *it* was.

I slipped through brush made anemic by the moonlight, disturbing a grasshopper who rode the top of a shaft of grass. At a break in the scrub, I saw them: Binky, ten yards from shore at four o'clock if I was at six, trying to elude a man who kept reaching for her. Then another form on the bank at three o'clock, pulling off his shoes and diving in—David, trying to reach her.

Madam was in the water, lunging forward, springing back, lunging, barking, at four-thirty: Rosellen had lost hold of her lead.

Ray was somewhere at what should be about eleven o'clock, soon to set upon the man who caused the night to tear apart.

The path I had to take to avoid being seen from the ridge lost me my sight-line to the water. I came out at a clearing near the bank some thirty yards from Madam. Rosellen had the sense to hide herself low behind a tree. There was a fury of splashing, and now I saw David struggling with the man in the water. The guy socked David on the back of the neck. He dunked face forward in the water, then struggled to rise.

I saw the assailant's face. Hector Lizzaraga. He reached out and pulled Binky up out of the water by the hair, her gasps like the sucking heaves of an ocean. "Back off! I'll drownd her. I'll drownd the fucking bitch!"

"Leave her alone!" Dave shouted.

Lizzaraga cranked an arm around Binky's neck and walked her backward in the water. They rose on what must have been an underwater hump, then rapidly sank lower. She slipped and splashed down. Lizzaraga lost his grip.

Blam-blam! A cop's shot, a double-tap. Ray.

Lizzaraga flew back, caving into the water.

Madam, sprung crazy and brave with her own hoarse fear, crashed forward into the water, her leash leaping like a snake being dragged to death. Tearing out from behind the tree, Rosellen called, *"Noweta!* Madam, *Noweta!"*

David stumbled for Binky and lifted her out of the water. He dragged her to shore, glancing back to see if the hated form would rise again. Izzy did lift his face from the water, hovered there, moaning, and tried to inch forward and away from Madam, who turned sharply in her paddling then to follow Binky.

I didn't understand at first when I heard Ray's voice call out, "Put the gun down, *now!"*

"Que mosca te pico? What's the matter, *compadre?* I got no problem with you." It was Julio! The little guy. Now I saw them. Ray was crouched, gun leveled in the direction of the ridge. Julio glided along the ridgetop toward a stand of brush.

"Stand up and die or lay down and live! Your choice, bud!" Ray said, moving forward now. He spoke in Spanish again, the guy who didn't know Spanish, enough so I knew he had identified himself as an officer.

"I'm on him too," I said.

Julio called out, *"El pito! Lui e una merda!"*

Ray's flashlight clicked on, the beam cutting across the void. At last Julio's arms slowly raised. "Don't shoot!" he cried in a high-pitched voice. We saw the gun fall to the ground.

David and Binky sat on the porch, she with her red sweater on and he with the blue blanket thrown around his shoulders, repeating "It's going to be all right."

Lizzaraga lay inside, cuffed and quaking from cold and pain and fear. Piled onto his face was a wet T-shirt from Julio. Julio had caught him with a round from a .25, a Saturday-night special like we found in the hand of the Nellie Gail victim. He fired low, and he fired twice because the first one scared him. The projectile skated on the water, losing momentum, bounced, broke bone at the supraorbital, then cut across the nasal bone. It bled like a son-of-a-gun even after Lizzaraga submerged himself in the water.

Julio also wore cuffs, brought from Ray's truck. He said he was sick of it all, sick of Izzy and Greg and the whole business. When he saw the struggle in the water he tried to help.

"You had your hands around a gun, pal. You're toast," Ray said, and Julio began to cry. Don't send me back, he kept saying.

Ray was relentless. While we waited for deputies and emergency technicians he yelled in their faces, asking for *me,* about *my* Does found behind buildings, in culverts, by water tanks, under rocks. But neither one gave an answer. Several times Ray threatened to smack them, Izzy glaring and Julio pleading with his eyes but saying no more.

CHAPTER 30

Three weeks after violent events at Oso Lake—that polluted body of water named for a bear though the biggest animal around for many a year had been Madam—I was in my car headed for Camp Pendleton, the marine base at Oceanside.

Along the freeway shoulders, golden California poppies shook violently in the crosswinds. Inland, the smoky-green leaves of Peruvian pepper trees and a shrub named Texas Rangers broke the stark lines of hills. I passed the yellow signs stamped with silhouettes of a family fleeing across the lanes. In daylight they looked different, but still read *Prohibido*.

Don't run. Don't defy the lanes.

Greg Cheng had run. Cheng took a flier all right, but not before I shot into action and raised Boyd Russell from bed and said if he wanted to get the sheriff's "Attaboy" big-time, here was his chance: Wake a judge and get a phone warrant to confiscate Cheng's files. Cheng didn't try to access his funds until that next afternoon, and that's all the time we needed. His accounts were frozen. He tried it from a remote location, having enough sense not to return to his apartment, but we had him.

Sort of. He could not be located by either of the two case investigators. That sickened David. David kept saying, "He's *out* there," striking the heel of his hand on his leg. And we would say we knew, we knew, but he'd be brought up yet, on whatever, whenever.

I turned into the guard gate at Pendleton and gained admittance from a peach-fuzz youth in combat boots and khaki, then took a road past signs reading TANK XING, TROOP CROSSING, and BATTLE SIMULATION CENTER. Camouflage nets hung over tents, tanks, and other military vehicles nested in pull-outs from the road.

I drove by a sign pointing the way to Cockleburr Beach, outpacing a cadre of bicyclists outfitted in glow-in-the-dark riding outfits and half-shell helmets. A crow in my path nearly stood on its beak in a puddle to go after something tasty.

The low-lying hills opened then to a wide area that held a couple dozen cars, and to a plowed field beyond. I parked near a flank of circus trees, then got out my hat, shovel, and a five-gallon bucket, and slipped on my sunglasses against the glare of sun even through the overcast.

At the sign-up table I learned a prize was offered to anyone hauling in more than 300 pounds, six sacks, of potatoes. Ribbons would be awarded for the weirdest and biggest spud. The judging table already carried some that looked like Rocky Graziano. When a small girl ran up giggling to put another buttery yellow spud on the table, a volunteer took a crayon and wrote the child's name on a card to set in front. Most potatoes were the size of a racquetball. One with a three-legged growth on the bottom was labeled "Potatoe with an E."

I got instructed to watch for "seed" potatoes, which would rot a whole sack, and was shown a sample with that affliction: one with numerous white eyes. Beware of wet potatoes or black ones, she said, or ones with lots of eyes and little feet too. From a hook drilled into a table edge I peeled off three red mesh sacks, then moved off to a row. The plants were about two feet high. Their dark-green leaves were wilting from withheld irrigation after the first picking was over.

Trial and error taught me how far from the plant I could dig without cutting into starchy flesh. The soil was dry and the digging not easy. It would take some time to pick a hundred-pound sack. My method was to fill my plastic tub, then pour it in the tow sack.

Deep in the wide field, a tractor trailed a double flank of children with bouncing buckets, who leapt to see who could be first to get at the upheaved plants with golden nuggets hanging from the roots. The tractor and plow were a queer creation made of spare parts notable by different-colored metals. As it crept nearer my line of sight, I saw it was driven by a man whose skin was the hue of weak coffee and whose hair, when he removed his straw hat to wipe a band of sweat away, showed a shade lighter than the silver sky. An old man, a Hispanic man, leading children with a plow.

I thought of the young men for a time known as Juan Does, each lying desolate in outdoor venues and then in coroner's rooms. Each could have been one of these children only a few years back, or one day a weathered old man doing a good day's work for charity. For some of us now they would merely remain a cutting waste of vigor, lust, dreams, and promise gone astray.

Without the sun breaking through, still the sky grew bright with fiercest glare. Sweat prickled my skin and ran in rivulets under my shirt. I stood to let whatever breeze there was catch me, and gazed across what seemed like miles of better rows: always, there are greener fields. I stooped again for my bucket and red sack and dragged the weight along, painting a body track. I chose a new row, then scraped away a hole to set my teetery bucket in.

My thoughts went to Madam then, furiously pawing under an oak tree when I visited Rosellen's home a few days after the Oso Lake affair. The hound had gone so deep only her tail and rear flanks could be seen. When she came out for a breather, her muzzle was a weighted, hanging clot of mud.

"She does that when she's happy," Rosellen said. Rosellen had just come back with the dogs from a training lesson. She had a friend lay trail in O'Neill Regional Park, then let it get tramped on all day and took Madam and Mitzi out that afternoon. They found her friend in thirty minutes. "Now I can't stop this one from digging," she said, patting Madam's rear. I looked over at the other dog, Mitzi. She was the pale color of the inside of a clamshell and sat with her forelegs crossed, drooling over her water dish while Madam dug. Rosellen forgave me for getting her into a scary situation. Wanted to know when we could do it again.

When we had left the lake that night, Ray filed against Julio for unlawful possession and discharge of a firearm. He filed against Lizzaraga on General Principles, he said. The watch commander, of course, would have none of that, so Ray put Lizzaraga down on trespass on county-owned land till we could come up with something better. I told the WC that two investigators from Homicide would want to be interviewing this pair.

Investigators Boyd Russell and Will Bright kept after Julio. Julio said he suspected, even believed that Izzy had killed Nita. But Julio didn't know how *horribly* he'd killed her. Not until Will Bright showed him the crime scene photos did Julio roll over on Lizzaraga. In time, Julio Hermosa fingered Hector Lizzaraga for Juan Does 1, 2, 3, and 4 . . . as well as Juanita Ramona Coresta Estevez. Now Will Bright was working on a warrant to obtain a dental impression from Lizzaraga to compare with bite marks on Nita Estevez. Lizzaraga was a conscienceless *lagarto*, a lizard whose blood ran cold in his veins along with regular infusions of cocaine. Julio said Lizzaraga killed another boy in Mexico who was only eleven years old, claiming it was an accident. Julio wept when he said he believed him much longer than he should have.

Eventually the young man on the hill by the water tanks in Nellie Gail Ranch was formally identified as Carlos Sarmiento, half-brother to Victor Minor Montalvo, the San Juan Doe with the good haircut, and to Angela in the cantina. Carlos had been in love with Nita Estevez, same as Froylan Cordillo from Turtle Rock had, who brought her a rack of stolen rubbers to save her from AIDS. Hector Lizzaraga could not stand it, this fawning over a female. But why would the lizard go this far? Ask the wind. Ask the trailing moon. Maybe it was because she came to resist his efforts to prostitute her. Or maybe he despised her because she was loved by men he wanted to control.

In a plastic bag under the seat of a car Lizzaraga boosted from the UCI campus, the detectives found another ditch gun like the one Julio fired that night at the lake. They also found a .40-caliber Sig with DNA material on it from the victim at Nellie Gail. All the guns traced back to white owners who'd had their homes burglarized. The .44 Cheng waved at us that night was found in the brush. It belonged to his uncle, who, it turned out, was a police officer in Temple City, east of L.A.

Will and Boyd spent two weeks drawing linkages between Greg Cheng's enterprises and the illegals placed at two garment factories, a computer chip maker, and a company manufacturing disk drives and pressed CD's. That last was a business in Technology Park, near the building where Desi Cono Blanco, "Whitey," was found.

On the last Friday of the month, sleepy Investigator Russell was called into the sheriff's office, the Big Kahuna himself. Boyd thought he was due for a commendation. What he left with was a red-face and a notice of transfer. Rumor had it that he had slept late once too often, and Cliff Yaroshak, Chief Coroner, came home early from a trip one day to find Boyd's car in the driveway and his shirttails flying out the back door.

My sack was bulging with little faces peering out through the red mesh. I wondered how I'd get it over to the tables, heavy as it was. I looked to see who might help. In the row next to me was a black man with only one arm. Next to him was a beefy, bald man in a black T-shirt with a blue tattoo on his neck. Maybe the big guy was a prisoner on work furlough, or a biker with a big heart. Unfairly, looking at the beefer I recalled an incident two years back when a man walked down the strawberry rows, went up to one of the pickers and fired three rounds in his heart. Then he sprinted to the road to a waiting truck and was gone.

I stood my shovel in the ground to the hilt and slipped one of my gloves over the handle for a marker, then hied slowly over the humped rows to the coordinating center. Nearby, some of the pickers now sat on overturned buckets eating lunches.

What'll I do, I asked, with my full sack too heavy for me to lift? A hundred pounds of dead weight was more than I imagined. The volunteer told me I could leave it in the rows, just stand it up so it could be seen. A little boy ran up with a potato that looked like a teddy bear. With great joy he placed it on the judging table, then brushed his hand over it tenderly as if it were alive.

Back at my row, I drank from my camo jug and watched the sea of light-colored shirts move in the rows like gulls foraging on a beach.

I bent to my task again, and found myself humming a song

from the Linda Ronstadt album I'd bought for Joe.

So long ago . . . Joe at home with me on the balcony, Joe nuzzling my neck.

I let tears fall one-two, one-two onto the ripped roots of potato plant. I fingered all the harder through the clods in search of the white bulbs and imagined the spent tears giving back life.

What'll I do, when you . . . are far . . . away . . . ?

What'll I do . . . ? What'll I do . . . ?

For Joe did not make it home that Monday following the lake incident. Joe didn't make it home at all.

What'll I do-o-o when you are far away . . . ?

Potatoes clunked in the bottom of my blue bucket one handful at a time. I tossed thirteen spuds in from that one plant, and moved on to the next.

I once heard that people with chronic pain don't get stronger by it but weaker—that fewer degrees of pain brought more and more concession. I thought of my neighbor, Mrs. Langston, with her creative pummels to beat back pain brought on by muscle disease; of Trudy Kunitz and the punishing psychic pain she now endures. And of Binky Jalindo, sitting next to David in the inset for family at the chapel where the memorial service for Joe Sanders was held. How she kept crossing herself as the minister moved slowly in his white-and-purple robe to and fro.

The week following the service, David and "Tamika" Maureen Modesto Conaty took Binky to the store, bought her two suitcases and filled them with all the clothing she wanted, then watched her get on the Metrolink at the San Juan Capistrano station, to go back to Mexico to live with her parents and small brothers. There she would return to work in one of the thousands of *maquiladoras* along the border, assembling goods for export to the U.S., or paging through redeemed coupons delivered for counting from America's grocery stores. In her suitcase were ten fearsome figures from the Dinosaur Corps for the boys.

I thought of how David seemed to grow calmer and older and stronger all at once with a grace that seemed to look on everything with new eyes. He was changing his major, he said, going into law enforcement if they'd have him, and maybe, after a stint there, medicine.

In the days that followed, Gil Vanderman called, left messages on the machine I never answered. I do not know if one day I'll pick up his card again. Right now it has a ragged corner where the guinea pig clipped it. But I did not throw it away. It's under a pewter paperweight in the form of a Tasmanian carnivore.

By my bedside is a framed photo of Joe, an outdoor shot, as he was lifting his arms, going, "Squawk!," speaking Pterodactyl.

Going home that spud-digging day, I watched the green sea off to my left roister and jump in its little pitches as if skipping shells to the beach. I slowed at the checkpoint where the government sign said STOP HERE/U.S. OFFICERS and got waved through, safe beneath blonde hair, I guessed.

It troubled me that it seemed that not one single thing I did professionally helped to corner a despicable creep like Hector Lizzaraga; that the solution fell into place, the answers revealed because of the tortured emotions of a twenty-year-old who made a recoverable mistake. Today there is no Joe to commend me on smaller motions I have made to add substance to other cases. No Joe to kid or tell my troubles to.

By the time I reached San Clemente a thumbnail moon could be seen in the pale blue sky, that odd phenomenon that cast day-for-night in unlikely partnership, as I cast loss with gain in my heart. For I had known one of the best of men, failed one of the best, loved the best, lost the best—not just this one but one other, my Oakland Blue—and garnered the best through memories to tell my troubles to.

I flew along I-5 at a clip that would get a CHP officer on my tail shooting his tri-lights at me, and watched the cars heading south, surf boards nosing out windows, bicycles up-ended and strapped on car roofs, tires wildly spinning, beating the speed of the wind.